W9-BRW-776

"*Rat Rule 79* is a labyrinth of beauty, curiosity, and all things strange. Galchen effortlessly captures the chaos of being a thirteen-year-old girl; Fred is wild, half feral, both lost and found. I needed this book when I was a girl. I need this book as an adult. I will need this book when I am one hundred and thirteen."

—Laura Graveline, Brazos Bookstore (Houston, TX)

"Rivka Galchen's *Rat Rule 79* is clever and strange and so very much fun, but what makes *Rat Rule 79* so remarkable is the warmth and wisdom that exudes from its pages. A subversive *Wizard of Oz* for kids too smart for their own good, it's sure to become many a young readers' favorite book for years to come."

—David Gonzalez, Skylight Books (Los Angeles, CA)

"A smart, witty through-the-looking-glass journey about a thousand unusual, interesting things and all the big important ones, too: home, friendship, holding on, letting go, and growing up."

—Nicole Krauss, author of
The History of Love and *Great House*

"I really enjoyed this book because of the non-stop humor and interesting/diverse characters. Fred is a girl who has had to move many times because of her mom's work. When she moves to Twin Falls, ID, she stumbles upon a glowing lantern that ultimately leads her to a unique world where time is outlawed and no birthday parties are allowed. . . . This story was full of adventure and wacky chapter headings, too."

—Alex, age 10, City of Asylum Bookstore
Young Readers Board (Pittsburgh, PA)

"Witty, clever, and bright, *Rat Rule 79* is a timeless adventure for readers of all ages. Filled with logic problems, riddles, and sharp wordplay, the Land of Impossibility is a place you will want to visit again, and again, and again. The characters are vibrant and unique, the prose is snappy and engaging, and the illustrations are whimsical."

—Holly Roberts, Out West Books (Grand Junction, CO)

"Just beneath the surface story—which is chock-full of puzzles, jokes, antics, absurdities, and other delights—its heroine, the intrepid Fred, navigates a spiritual education in grief and love. Rivka Galchen has produced a book that somehow both sparkles and looms. *Rat Rule 79* is an absolute treasure."

—Sarah Manguso, author of *300 Arguments*

"It has all the joys of *The Phantom Tollbooth* and *Alice in Wonderland*. It playfully exposes the holes in logic as presented through language. That sounds too snooty. It's silly and deep at the same time with fun conundrums to ponder far beyond the last page."

—Philipp Goedicke, Community Bookstore (Brooklyn, NY)

"Galchen creates an impossible land, filled with some charming creatures that help a 12-year-old girl find the right way to get back home. Danger and unreason are defeated by logic and love. Original and beautiful illustrations by Elena Megalos."

—Pamela Pescosolido, The Bookloft (Great Barrington, MA)

RAT RULE 79

ALSO BY RIVKA GALCHEN

Atmospheric Disturbances: A Novel
American Innovations: Stories
Little Labors: Essays

RAT RULE 79

AN ADVENTURE

Rivka Galchen

Illustrations by
ELENA MEGALOS

Restless Books
for Young Readers

First Restless Books hardcover edition September 2019

Hardcover ISBN: 9781632060990
Library of Congress Control Number: 2018956685

Cover design by Aubrey Nolan
Cover illustration by Elena Megalos
Set in Carre Noir by Tetragon, London

Printed in China

1 3 5 7 9 10 8 6 4 2

Restless Books, Inc.
232 3rd Street, Suite A101
Brooklyn, NY 11215

restlessbooks.org
publisher@restlessbooks.org

To the girl whose mother is my mother's girl

Contents

RAT RULE 79

Chapter Zero

Not long ago and not far away, in fact right here in the living room, there was a girl named Fred. Fred was not being chased by wolves. She was not battling an intergalactic clan of space pirates. She did not have ESP, she could not levitate, she was not an expert swordswoman, and she did not eat lightning. You might say Fred was a pretty normal girl—even if her favorite sandwich was peanut butter and pickles on raisin bread.

Even if nothing unusual had ever happened to her, I would care deeply about Fred. I would care about her simply because she was, and is, Fred.

Yet some unusual things did happen.

Chapter Tuesday

On a not particularly recent Tuesday night, Fred's mom was setting the table: two paper plates on a red-and-white check tablecloth. Fred and her mother were getting ready to eat takeout lo mein noodles—a happy fact, according to Fred. Fred's mom was using paper plates because Fred and her mother were in yet another new apartment in yet another new city—an unhappy fact. In the last six years, Fred and her mom had lived in Wichita, Kansas; Boulder, Colorado; Iowa City, Iowa and Norman, Oklahoma. This was their first night in Twin Falls, Idaho.

Fred was sick of paper plates. She was sick of boxes, sick of packing and unpacking and repacking. She was bothered by everything about this bare and unfamiliar new room except her mother and the familiar red-and-white check tablecloth—the tablecloth that had traveled everywhere with them.

But still, the noodles were a happy fact. That was undeniable. According to Fred's Unwritten Rule Book for Living, there were two Truly Great Meals. The first was the aforementioned peanut butter and pickle sandwich, especially when made with raisin bread. Wherever Fred's home was, and however bare it was, she could almost always count on some peanut butter, some pickles, and some bread. They were her true friends.

The second Truly Great Meal was takeout lo mein noodles, because aside from being ultra-scrumptious, they always came with fortune cookies. Wherever Fred and her mom lived, they always managed to find a nice place to get takeout noodles. Noodles were also Fred's true friends.

Fred took a deep breath, sat down, and resolved to be nice about being in the new apartment, in the new town.

Then her mother said: "What should we do for your birthday?"

Should I have mentioned this earlier? This particular Tuesday was the day before Fred's 13th birthday.

Fred's mom went on: "I thought maybe we could throw a party in a week or two, once the school year has started, since by then you'll have some friends—"

"No," Fred said.

"We'll still do something tomorrow, just you and me. But—"

"No," Fred said. "No party. Not tomorrow. Not in a few weeks. Not in the mood."

Her mom smoothed the check tablecloth with her blue-veined hand. Finally she said, "I like that. No more birthdays. No more getting older."

"That's a dumb joke," Fred mumbled. The noodles still tasted delicious. But as the ensuing silence between Fred and her mother grew longer, each noodle began to taste of a question. Why did her mom always just *tell* her they were moving? Didn't she think she should ask her, Fred, if she wanted to move? She wasn't a houseplant, she was a person. And even houseplants might have feelings. What did math professors—supposedly her mom's job—really do all day?

Why did her mom wear her hair in a ponytail so often? Why did she never buy Fred the correct size of clothes? Why was the phrase "birthday suit" so blech? Why had they never owned a cat?

These were angry questions, you will have noticed.

Fred said, "We never do anything for *your* birthday. I don't even know when your birthday is."

Her mom was picking at the last few snap peas and carrots among the noodles. "October 29th," she said.

"Strange," Fred said.

"What's strange about the 29th of October? The 79th of October, now that would be a strange birthday."

"It's strange that your birthday date doesn't even sound familiar to me," said Fred.

They glumly finished off their delicious noodles.

"Fortune cookie time?" her mom said.

As everyone knows, the best of part of a fortune cookie isn't the cookie itself. It's what's written inside, on the strip of paper, in delicate red letters. Except when the inside message is boring, like lottery numbers, or advice about being kind.

"You read first," Fred said to her mom.

Her mom unfolded the slip of paper: "THANK YOU FOR GETTING ME OUT OF THERE!"

"Weird," Fred said.

"Your turn," her mom said.

Fred's fortune cookie message was even weirder. She read out loud: "LIFE IS TWO LOCKED BOXES, EACH CONTAINING THE OTHER'S KEY."

"Two locked boxes?"

"That's what it says."

"Huh. That's odd. Though it sounds familiar somehow."

"It's not even a fortune!" Fred complained. "Even the fortune cookies in this town are annoying."

Her mom started clearing the table. Fred didn't help. Her mom said, "You're tired. You'll feel better after you sleep. It's amazing how many problems are solved by sleep."

Sleep! What a dumb suggestion. Sleep was just a kind of nothingness. How could a few hours of nothingness solve anything? Another entry in Fred's Unwritten Rule Book for Living was that *sleep* as a solution to anything was one of the Two Most Useless Solutions. The other most useless solution was Knowing That You're Loved. If Fred were to ask her mom what two plus seven was, Fred was sure her mom would answer either Sleep, or Know That I Love You So Much.

"I'm *not* tired," Fred said. "And you're ignoring the elephant in the room: I have nothing and nobody here."

"Well, that's two things—Nothing and Nobody," Fred's mom joked, her back to Fred. She was tying up the trash. She turned back toward Fred and said gently, "Know that I love you so much, Fred."

"I knew you would say that," Fred said bitterly.

"Tomorrow will be a better day."

Fred laughed a small, unhappy laugh. "My birthday, you mean?"

Her mom said nothing.

7

"Good night then," Fred said in a fury. And she stormed off to her small, near-empty new bedroom, where there was only a mattress on the floor and her old moon-shaped night-light plugged into the wall. There she sat, wide-awake, cross-legged, and very, very mad.

Chapter Red

Dear reader, perhaps you've been conscripted into the Sleep War. It's a war between those who despise sleep (most kids) and those who are devoted to sleep (just about every adult.) Which is backward if you think about it, since adults are the ones who consistently tell perfectly awake kids to go to sleep while they themselves, the supposedly sleep-worshipping adults, stay up and up and up. I won't mention which side of the Sleep War I'm on, in part because there are ways to be on both sides of a line at once, for example, by being the line.

But back to the point. Fred thought her mom's advice to get some sleep was so wrong, and so clueless, and so infuriating, and so. . . . Well, the very thought of it kept Fred awake. Awake and angry. So awake and so angry that she resolved that she definitely would not sleep until her mom came into her room and apologized to her. Oh, yes. She would wait for her mother to walk into her (new, small, empty, horrible) bedroom and say *Sorry*. Right there in the wavering glow of the night-light moon. Fred was willing to wait forever for her mother to apologize to her for the dumb idea that sleep (or love, or whatever) would make her feel better. And maybe for other things, too. For the irritating seam on her socks. For the way humidity made her ears feel itchy. For the name "Fred." For the excruciating-ness of introducing one's self, over and over and—

Chapter Redder

However: Fred's mom continued not coming into Fred's room to apologize. What was she doing out there? Did she expect Fred to stay up nearly forever waiting, like a giraffe? (Fred knew that giraffes sleep only about thirty minutes a day, standing up.) It was so quiet out there. Weirdly quiet. Was her mom staring at a computer screen again? Doing her "work"?

Often Fred was right when she made guesses about what her mom was doing, just as she was often right when she made guesses as to what her mom was going to say. They knew each other very, very well, even though an adult and a child are like two different species. On this particular evening, though, Fred was wrong.

I'm a fan of being wrong. At least now and again. Being wrong is often the first sign that you're about to learn something new. You might say that being wrong is the first step of an adventure. Or you might say that this is the kind of irritatingly chipper and totally unconvincing thing Fred's mom might say.

Fred opened the door and saw her mom in the living room. (Not surprising.) Standing with her back to Fred. (A little bit surprising that she was standing up, almost as if at attention.) Staring at an enormous white paper lantern. (That was a very big bit surprising, the paper lantern part.) Fred had never seen this lantern before, or any lantern of its kind. The lantern reached nearly to the ceiling and was even wider than it was high. It reminded Fred of that accordion paper you get after scrunching down the wrapper of a straw. You scrunch down the straw wrapper, then drip a drop of water on it and watch the wrapper grow, like a magic paper snake. Why was Fred thinking about *that* at a time like this?

"Hey!" Fred called out.

Her mom didn't hear her.

Her mom, Fred noticed, was wearing a floor-length red-and-white check skirt, as if she were headed to some fancy party. Or to a picnic. One or the other. Unless it was both. At that moment, as Fred was thinking that her mom's clothing made her look like a kid dressed up as an adult, it finally crossed Fred's mind to be concerned. Even scared. Her mom seemed under the sway of . . . something. And then her mom stepped into the lantern. Not *through a door* in the lantern, but right *through* the lantern. She stepped in, and then was gone.

Chapter 12^{364}/$_{365}$

The thing about being twelve (and very nearly thirteen) is that you're old enough to look after your mom. How often had her mom forgotten to plan for dinner and Fred had saved the day with peanut butter and pickle sandwiches? How often had Fred's mom misplaced her keys, or her wallet, and relied on Fred to find them? Fred had taken care of her mom before, and she could do it again.

But the other thing about being twelve is that you don't always take a good look around you. You don't always take a deep breath and have a little think before making a decision.

Never mind, those are not things about being twelve, those are things about being human, at any age. Don't let anyone tell you otherwise.

What I'm saying is, Fred made a decision she would later regret. She touched the lantern's edge; she stepped forward; and that was that. Or perhaps I should say, that was this:

The Surprising
Dungeon Chapter
Without Assigned
Number

D id I mention that Fred was wearing fluffy bunny slippers? And planet pajamas? Which was perfectly fine for going to sleep but would not be Fred's preferred attire for social appearances. Fred found herself, in her pajamas and slippers, in a small, sunny room. Or rather, it was a damp and dark room with a small high window that let in the light. The room looked just like what Fred imagined a dungeon looked like, in those stories where people keep finding themselves in dungeons, often with a pile of hay in the corner. Why hay? As if dungeons were places for badly behaved horses. Anyhow, coming through that window were those rays of sunshine that can make a window seem like a portal to another world. If you're in that kind of mood.

"Well, this is surprising," Fred said aloud to herself.

"Nice slippers," said another voice.

"Thanks, I don't usually—" Then she was confused and embarrassed and looking around for the source of the voice.

"But you're wrong to say this is surprising," the voice continued. "Unfortunately, this place is *not* surprising." The voice sighed. "Not surprising at all."

The voice was an elephant's. I mean, Fred thought she saw an elephant in the room's dark corner, though the brightness from the window made it difficult to make out the shape. There was a fluffy paleness that wavered between resembling a rumpled sheet and a whitish elephant, but the shape eventually settled into a whitish elephant. A smallish, whitish elephant. Though still at least twice the size of Fred.

The at-once-small-and-large creature said: "*Nothing* is surprising here. And that's the problem."

Fred looked around the supposedly unsurprising room. It was the size of her bedroom, but with stone walls, a stone door, and penny-colored prison bars in the one high window. It smelled like a well-kept stable. Several fliers were pasted onto the wall, including one that read WANTED: ALIVE OR ALIVE and displayed the anxious face of a young deer. "How long have you been here?" Fred asked.

"I don't keep track of time," the elephant said.

"You mean you've been here so long that you've lost track of time?"

"No, I don't mean that." The elephant sighed one of those trunky, ear-flapping, head-shaking sighs that only elephants can do properly. "I don't keep track of time because it's *illegal*. Aren't you familiar with Rat Rule 79?"

With his trunk, the elephant indicated one of the fliers pasted on the wall:

16

THE ESSENTIAL AND VERY GOOD AND NO ONE CAN DISAGREE WITH
RAT RULE 79

☞ *NO WORKING CLOCKS*
☞ *NO TICKS OR TOCKS*
☞ *NO HOURGLASSES*
☞ *NO EGG TIMERS*
☞ *NO SUNDIALS*
☞ *NO GETTING OLDER*
☞ *NO GETTING WISER*
☞ *NO CHANGING A HAIR ON ONE'S HEAD*

. . . .

The list went on and on, in tinier and tinier script. Fred gave up before reaching the end. "At least it doesn't say 'No peanut butter,'" Fred said.

"Oh, that's on there, too. Right after 'No being unkind to camels.'"

"Really?"

The elephant blinked; his eyelashes were long and beautiful. "Once you start banning things, you can get carried away, even if you're the Rat Queen of Rightness and Reasonability and Radial Tires and Runless Stockings and Seedless Watermelons and so on."

Fred looked at the flier. The list ended with one last prohibition, in boldface and again large letters:

AND ABSOLUTELY
NO BIRTHDAY PARTIES

And No Saying the Phrase 'Birthday Party'
or Any Other Phrase Referring Directly or
Indirectly to the Celebration of an Anniversary of
the Day on Which Anyone Was Born.

This Rule Constitutes the Last
Permissible Use of the Term 'Birthday Party.'

"Wow. Great rule," Fred said.

She meant it sarcastically, of course. Saying the opposite of what you mean is an understandable method of communication most of the time. But the elephant sounded entirely serious when he replied: "Yes, The Essential and Very Good and No One Can Disagree with Rat Rule 79 is the last of what we call the Late and Great Rules of the Rat's Rule Book for Living."

"Oh," said Fred.

Energized, the elephant began to explain: "To fully appreciate Rat Rule 79, you have to understand the Rat's Late, Great Argument." The elephant pulled out a red umbrella from it wasn't clear where and began a brief, animated lecture. "Firstly, Children are the Best Thing in the World. Secondly, given that Children are the Best Thing in the World, it follows that They Shall Not Be Allowed to Get Older—because then they would cease to be children. Thirdly, since Children don't want to be the only ones not getting older, No One

Else Is Allowed to Get Older either. For the sake of the Children. QED: The Essential and Very Good and No One Can Disagree with Rat Rule 79." He gave a proud, elephanty bow and set the umbrella down.

Well, Fred had no idea what to say in response to that.

She was *tempted* to point out that you can't keep people from getting older just by telling them they're not allowed to. That was like saying all number sevens must be friendly. Or that all blue must be heavy. But Fred kept these thoughts to herself because she was well accustomed to being in new settings, where you never knew how people (or elephants) might respond. Generally, people didn't like a naysayer. "I should have introduced myself," Fred said simply. "I'm Fred."

"That's reasonable," the elephant said. "I'm Downer. That's not my real name. But that's what my friends call me. Or what they would call me, if I had friends. Which I don't. Because I'm such a downer. Maybe I'm such a downer because I have no friends."

"You seem very nice," Fred said. "I like your red umbrella."

Downer said, "It's the one good thing about me, right?"

Chapter Together

Tigers prefer to live on their own, sharks sometimes eat their own babies, but elephants—elephants laugh, they cry, they mourn their dead. Grown-up elephants have been known to adopt orphan elephants. You can sing an elephant to sleep with a lullaby. Really. Elephants are social, family creatures. But Downer was all alone. Until Fred arrived. Downer didn't say it, nor did he even admit it to himself, but Fred's arrival had lifted his spirits.

"Are you a child?" Downer asked.

"Sort of," Fred answered. "Part child. Part grown-up."

"You must be one or the other," Downer said. "The slippers made me think you were a child. They're really great slippers." Then Downer reiterated, "Children Are the Best Thing in the World."

Fred shrugged.

"It's nice to be near a child. Being here hasn't been easy. But I suppose this is what happens to someone who does nothing wrong." Downer began to tell Fred about himself. "I supported the Rat Queen because she was always right. I supported her because she was the Rattiest of Rats—the most righteous, the most rational, the inventor of rockets, the discoverer of quarks. Many were angry when she passed THE ESSENTIAL AND VERY GOOD AND NO ONE CAN DISAGREE WITH RAT RULE 79. But not me!

I figured that if she made that Rule, she made it *for a reason.*
Everything happens for a reason. At least it used to, when the
Rat was in charge. I love the Rat so much. I hope she knows
that. Do you think she knows?"

Fred elected not to mention that, where she was from,
rats were not revered creatures.

Downer went on, "Whatever Rule the Rat Queen made,
I respected. She was right, righteous, and rational. She knew
how to make gummy bears and gliders and . . . you get the
point. I guess I should also confess that she once saved my life."

"A rat saved an elephant?"

"We'll get to that story," Downer said.

Fred took another look around the dungeon. Why was
Downer here? Why was she? Where was her mom? Would
there be snacks?

Downer spoke up again: "But first I have to ask you: are
you a supporter of the Rat Queen?"

Fred really wanted to be nice. "I would say—" She had
been known to say to the parents of kids whose homes she
had been invited to that sure, she would love an egg salad
sandwich, when really, an egg salad sandwich was a nightmare. It was better to be honest than agreeable, if you wanted
to avoid egg salad sandwiches and their like. The only rat
Fred had ever met belonged to her most recent Social Studies
teacher, Mr. Steele, and had been named Edison. Edison spent
a lot of time sleeping, though Mr. Steele claimed he was lively
at night. "Um, well, I've never even heard of the Rat," Fred
finally admitted. "I came here looking for my mom."

Downer gave Fred a long, assessing stare. "Your mom. Interesting." He tapped his red umbrella on the ground philosophically. "Well, the Rat is a mom. I assume she's not your mom. Though her being a mom does have something to do with what has happened here. You're obviously a newcomer. You seem very nice. You're bound to have questions. Shall I start by telling you my story?"

"Do you know my mom?" Fred asked quietly. "Did she come through here?"

Downer either ignored or didn't hear the questions. He began his tale.

Chapter Sixty-One

"Have you ever heard of The Elephant in the Room?" Downer asked. "Before the Rule of the Rat, most people obeyed the unwritten rule: Don't Mention the Elephant in the Room. Can you imagine what that was like? Being in a room with everyone ignoring you?"

Fred actually did know how that felt. It was like being the new girl in town.

"Have you ever tried to buy a bag of peanuts when no one sees you? Do you know what it's like to smile at someone and not get smiled at back? Or even worse, to scowl at someone and not get a scowl in return?"

"You couldn't even order lo mein noodles," offered Fred.

"Exactly. So, when I heard the Rat Queen was coming to visit my stomping ground, I thought: *Maybe she can help.* It was said of the Rat that she could Solve Any Problem. Because she was the most righteous, the most rational, the inventor of string cheese . . . you get the idea. I figured, why not try? But I was so nervous. I didn't know what to say. Or how to explain my problem. I was worried I would freeze up and say nothing. And then I wouldn't know if she was saying nothing to me because I had said nothing, or saying nothing to me because she wouldn't admit I was there." Downer paused. His face flushed pinkish.

"So what *did* you say?"

Downer took a deep breath. He extended his ears dramatically. "I said, 'Knock, knock.'"

"Knock knock?"

"Yep."

"Huh."

"Can you guess what happened next?"

"Um, did she say, 'Who's there?'"

Downer looked panicked. "Did someone already tell you my story? Who's been telling stories about me?"

"I was guessing," Fred said hastily. "I'm sorry. I shouldn't have guessed."

Downer took a deep breath and continued in a soft voice. "It was so meaningful to me to hear the Rat say *Who's there?* Because, you know, I *was* there. Even though I was the Elephant in the Room." Tears started forming on Downer's long eyelashes. "And then the Rat did even more for me. After learning of my plight—how no one saw me, how no one ever admitted I was there, she . . . she . . . she passed a Rule."

"A Rule?"

"Yes. A Rule. The Utterly Perfect Rat Rule 61. A Rule that said I was There." Downer showed her another flier:

THE UTTERLY PERFECT RAT RULE 61

When an elephant is in the room, all shall acknowledge that there is an elephant in the room. There shall be no not acknowledging the Elephant in the Room. When there is no Elephant in the Room, that also shall be acknowledged. We hereby reaffirm that elephants exist in some places, and at some times.

24

"Congratulations," Fred said.

"Yes," Downer said, wiping a happy tear. "It's quite moving."

"It's a nice story—"

"I agree," Downer sniffed.

"But it doesn't explain why you're here, or—"

Downer interrupted, "I haven't finished yet. I took a moment there because I got a bit emotional. Listen, even though, thanks to The Utterly Perfect Rat Rule 61, everyone had to acknowledge that I exist, the Rule couldn't make anyone like me. People tend to steer clear of a downer." He sighed. "Whereas in fact Downer is a beautiful name in the elephant world. That misunderstanding got me down even more. And I then truly did become more of a downer to have around. Which meant people had even more reason to not want to be my friend." He hung his head low. "The Rat did her best, but I'm still me. She's great. And I'm pathetic." He slumped down. "And no one loves me."

Fred felt like they were back at square one. How had she landed in a dungeon with a depressed elephant? It was just like her mom to dash off somewhere without telling her. "Downer," she said, "if the Rat is so great, then why are you, her super devoted follower, here? In . . . a dungeon?"

Downer's tears dried up. "It's not her fault. The Fearsome Ferlings caught the Rat and put her in the Bag. It's *their* fault. I'm here because I tried to let the Rat out of the Bag."

Lucky Numbers

That's when Fred decided she must be in a dream—a weird fortune-cookie induced dream.

"Let me get this straight," Fred said. "The Rat's in a bag? Which the Funky Feelings put her in?"

"Fearsome Ferlings."

"Okay, Fearsome Ferlings. And then when you tried to let the Rat out of the Bag . . . what happened?"

"Right. I remember seeing a little dog named Dogma, and then next thing I knew . . . I woke up in here. And the Rat can't get me out of this dungeon until I let her out of the Bag. And I can't get her out of the Bag until I'm out of this dungeon. And I can't get out of the dungeon until the Rat—you get the point." Downer sniffed sadly.

Fred found herself saying, "So it's sort of like two locked boxes, each containing the other's key?" She was now most definitely blaming the fortune cookies for this mess.

"That sounds familiar," Downer said, which itself sounded familiar to Fred.

It all felt like a problem Fred was supposed to solve. But the solution certainly wouldn't be A Good Night's Sleep or Knowing that She Was Loved. A memory of the THANK YOU FOR GETTING ME OUT OF THERE! fortune tickled at her. "I bet you mean Cat, not Rat," Fred announced. "I bet you mean you tried to let the *Cat* out of the bag." It was a simple case of swapping. Soon everything would be better. All the egg-salad sandwiches of the world would become peanut butter and pickle sandwiches. All the different places Fred had moved to and would have to move to again would become one single place. It would all work out. She would think it through. Clearly.

"Who puts a cat in a bag? That would be a very strange thing to do," Downer said with conviction.

"Conviction" is a funny word because it means both that you really believe something is true *and* that someone is officially guilty of a crime. Why did being certain of something have to share a word with putting someone in jail? Why couldn't it share a word with getting people *out* of jail? For instance, the jail Fred and Downer were in right then?

Fred looked again at the stone door and the penny bars in the window. The Rat Rule fliers, the Wanted Alive or Alive flier. Okay, she was in a locked room and she had no key. She started to chew on her nails. Which she did at times, to help her think. Her mom had once told her, when Fred was chewing her nails, that a human fingernail offered only sodium and two calories per nail. To her credit, unlike other mothers, Fred's mom had never scolded Fred to stop chewing her nails, since, after all, who did it hurt? Nobody—except occasionally Fred herself, when she bit off too much nail and exposed the nail bed. They call it a nail bed, even though no one and nothing sleeps on a nail bed, that soft red skin under a toenail or fingernail. No one lies on a nail bed, but she had heard of people lying on a *bed of nails*—

Fred stopped chewing. She had an idea: maybe to get out of this dungeon she had to *get out of bed*. She had to wake up!

"It's been very nice talking to you, Downer," Fred declared. "I've never spoken to a white elephant before, or any elephant, and it's exciting, and an honor. I don't usually like meeting new people, but I did like meeting you. Very much. I want you to know that. But I'm going to go ahead and go back home, okay? My mom is probably already there. That's my plan."

"Is this because you don't love me?" Downer asked. "I'm okay with that. I'm used to not being loved. I just want to understand."

Sleep solves all problems? Fred mused. *And so does Knowing that You're Loved?* Whatever! "Now how do I do this, Downer? Click my heels? Pinch myself? Wait for an alarm?"

"Are you hopeful?" Downer looked at Fred with tenderness. "Hope is so painful."

In the first of many illegal actions to come, Fred ignored the elephant in the room, thereby violating The Utterly Perfect Rat Rule 61. Closing her eyes, she took a deep, hay-steeped breath and whispered: Home, home, home, home, home, home.

Chapter Seven
Surprising
Days

If you are a certain kind of person, you'll be surprised to learn that Fred's strategy for escaping the dungeon did not work. If you are another kind of person, you will *not* be surprised. Most people start out as the first kind of person—full of hope—but eventually grow up into the plain old second kind—the kind that doesn't get surprised, and doesn't feel hope. Some folks believe that not being surprised—or at least not *admitting* to being surprised—is a sign of being grown up. I disagree with those people. But no one's asking for my opinion.

Fred thought she was the second, grown-up kind of person—but it turned out she was really the first kind. She *was* surprised. Another word for surprised is disappointed.

When Fred opened her eyes, she was still in her planet pajamas and fuzzy bunny slippers (comforting) and still in a dungeon with Downer (not so comforting). She was definitely not back home. Not even in her bland, new home with an enormous paper lantern in the middle of the living room, a paper lantern standing there with some kind of unreadable conviction, if something made out of paper can be said to have conviction.

Fred had conviction. She took off one of her slippers and threw it hard against a wall. "Drat and double drat!" she shouted. "Triple drat and drat, drat, drat!" This went on for a while.

"Don't be mad at the Rat," the elephant said finally. "We have the Fearsome Ferlings to blame. Be mad at the Ferlings!"

Fred didn't know (yet) what a Ferling was. But as the red fury passed, she started to feel a *feeling* that was not unlike the feeling of it being more than forty-five minutes since the school day has ended and still no one has arrived to pick you up. Fred sat on a pile of hay and leaned against Downer's broad and wrinkled leg. The sad face of the deer on the WANTED poster seemed to regard her with pity.

Downer said gently, "I know being here with me isn't what you want. Would it make you feel better if I told you that the Rat promised I would be freed within a week?"

Fred brushed hay off her planet pajamas, straightened her posture, wiped her eyes with her sleeve. "Why didn't you mention that before?"

"Because it's *not* going to happen," Downer said.

"You just said it *was* going to happen."

"What I said was that *the Rat* said it was going to happen."

Downer's eyelashes no longer looked beautiful to Fred, but instead like the bristles of an old dustpan brush. "You told me the Rat is always right, and righteous, and—"

"That is correct."

"But somehow she's wrong?"

"Incorrect."

The two of them were like characters in an equation proving that if you lock up two creatures in a small space, at some point they will begin to bicker like siblings. Or maybe that's not the equation—siblings, of course, would begin to bicker right away.

"Are you saying the Rat is not . . . reliable?" Fred asked. Reliable was a word Fred was attuned to because her mom, after being more than forty-five minutes late picking Fred up from school for the third day in a row, had promised to become more reliable. And later, when her mom had given her only a day's warning about switching schools, she had again said she would try to be more reliable.

"Oh, the Rat is perfectly *reliable*. I mean, she's the Rat of Reasoning and Rationality, of Rockets and Ribonuclease Inhibitors and . . . ." Downer twirled his bright umbrella briefly, but then set it back down. "You get the idea. She's *perfectly* reliable. And that's the problem."

"I'm losing track of what the problem is. I thought the Rat being held captive in the Bag was the problem."

"Nope."

"Or that nobody loves you?"

Downer shook his head again. In a dejected voice, he said, "Take a look for yourself." Downer showed Fred a handwritten note:

To the inestimably dear Downer,

Someone will come to release
you in the next seven days.

I Promise!

Which day it is will SURPRISE
you.

Again, I promise!

Yours in Utter Perfection,

RAT QUEEN

Fred smiled. "It's a little kooky, but this does make me feel more hopeful."

"You feel hopeful because you aren't thinking. Unfortunately, I excel at thinking."

"What's the problem now?" Fred asked.

"Think about it. The note says I'll be surprised by the day of my release. Got that?"

"Yes . . . . So?"

Downer shook his head, flapping his tremendous ears. "Think. I *know* that I won't be freed on the seventh day. How do I know this?" Using his umbrella, Downer scratched a chart into the dirt floor, with boxes around each of the numbers one to seven. "Because by the sixth day, I would *know* that I was going to be freed on the seventh day. Then the seventh day wouldn't be a surprise, right? The note clearly states that I will be surprised. So we can rule out Day Seven." He X-ed out the number seven box.

"Fine," Fred said. "There are still all the other days." Her stomach growled. She hoped it wouldn't be too long before a peanut butter and pickle sandwich presented itself.

"But if Day Seven is ruled out, then it can't be Day Six. Do you see why? We've ruled out Day Seven, so by Day Five, if I still haven't been freed, I would *know* it would be Day Six, so Day Six also wouldn't be a surprise. No Day Six." He X-ed out the Day Six box. "Once you've ruled out Days Six and Seven, you have to rule out Day Five, because it's now the Last Day, and being released on the Last Day will never come as a surprise. Same thing with Day Four. And Day Three, and so on. So *none* of the days can be surprising. Get it?"

"Not really. You're saying we're going to die in here because of a logic problem?"

Downer's voice grew angry. "If the Rat said it was going to be a surprise, it's definitely going to be a surprise. The Rat always means what she says."

"Maybe you're taking the surprise thing too seriously," Fred suggested. She wished her mom were here, so she and Downer could get help with the logic, or nonsense, of the Rat's note.

"No," Downer said flatly.

"Or there's been a mistake," Fred argued. "The Rat could have said *you guys* and whoever wrote it down for her misheard it as *surprise*. Or the Rat wanted to say *you will be pleased* but wrote *you will be surprised* because, well, maybe at that moment she was thinking of a side of *French fries.* . . . The possibilities are endless."

"Mm, yeah . . . I don't think so," Downer said. He drew a big, doleful X over his entire dirt diagram.

"You *are* a downer," Fred said. Then, with sudden energy, she exclaimed, "But hey—what about me?"

"You mean—*you're* the surprise?" Downer asked. "I *was* thinking—"

"No. I mean the letter doesn't say anything about *me*. Will someone come and get *me*?"

"Well, what did the Rat tell you?"

"The Rat didn't tell me anything! I told you I don't know the Rat, I've never spoken to the Rat. I've never spoken to *any* rat." (Except sleepy Edison, with whom she had actually shared a fair number of her troubles, but Edison never spoke back, so Fred figured that didn't count.) "I've never even spoken to an elephant before now. Let alone such a gloomy one. This is worse than moving to a new town. This is terrible. This is a *real* pickle."

"It's not a real pickle, it's a metaphorical pickle."

"You know what I mean—"

"But why say *real pickle* precisely when you mean *not a real* pickle, and—"

Fred and Downer began to panic, and to bicker, and to bicker more and panic more, arguing about what was or wasn't a pickle, and what was or wasn't surprising, and who was or wasn't going to be going where, and when, and how you can even count days when you can't keep track of time, and as they argued they were once again proving the equation about two creatures locked in a small room for long enough—

When there came a knock at the door. Or, you might even say, a Knock, Knock at the door.

Chapter Thirty Minutes

What happened next is close to unbelievable, but you can read about it if you want. Or you could not read about it. Unless someone is forcing you to read. But even then, even if you're being forced and they've set a timer by your bedside and you have to keep reading until it goes off, even then you could just turn the pages and pretend to read. I've done that before, and I wouldn't judge you. Another option would be to explain to the adult in question that the passage of time is an illusion. I don't know if it really *is* an illusion, but people seem willing to talk that over for pretty much ever. You distract them, in other words, and before you know it the time for reading will be over.

Real Pickles

"**I** surprised you, didn't I?" said a mongoose who was wearing jeans and a red "Workin' Hard" T-shirt and carrying a small orange backpack. On her neck hung seventeen golden lockets, which clinked cheerfully as she swung open the heavy door, letting in a loamy fresh breeze. Fred and Downer stepped out into a vast open green.

"Wow," Fred said.

"Pretty nice, right?" the mongoose said. "So, umm, is there a deer in here, too? I was expecting a deer. A youngish deer, cute little nubs for antlers. Seen anyone like that?"

Fred and Downer were too overwhelmed with their new freedom to take in the mongoose's inquiry. Seen from the outside, the dungeon they had been in looked as sweet as a little stone toolshed that might house a lawnmower, or an old kiddie pool and sprinklers. In the field before them, amidst the grasses, were countless purple and yellow wildflowers.

"I should have known there would be a solution," Downer said. "I'm always wrong." He started doing a heavy-footed soft-shoe dance with his umbrella, while he sang:

Oh thank you Ratty Rat-a-Tat-Tat
Ruling Rat
of Reason and Rationality
of Rockets and Pocket Calculators

and Freeze-Dried Ice Cream.
Thank you understander of Rainbows
and Rotating Crops
and Shiny Bits of Glass in Sidewalks
Oh Ratty-Rat-Rat, we love you,
Oh Ratty-Tat-Tat, we'll never shove you,
Except, maybe, by accident.

"Um, Downer, maybe you should thank this mongoose, too?" Fred said.

The mongoose clapped enthusiastically. "Great song! Great show!"

"Oh yes, thank you, of course," Downer said with a respectful bow. "You are a most worthy mongoose."

"I'm impressed that you know I'm a mongoose," said the mongoose, extending a paw. "Gogo's the name. Hate being called a meerkat. No disrespect to meerkats. And no need to thank me for the dungeon liberation. I'm happier than a hippo in mud to help. Happier than a mongoose getting out of a job fighting cobras. In fact, I *am* a mongoose getting out of fighting cobras. Absolutely delighted to oblige. I admit I thought there would be a deer in this dungeon, not an elephant and a girl. Yes, I did think and hope there would be a deer. But still happy to help." She pulled some papers out of a pocket and looked at Fred. "Nice bunny slippers, by the way. Does that mean you're a kid?" Gogo the mongoose took a seat on a stone near Fred and said, "I love kids. Would you like to see photos of *my* kids?"

Yes, Fred definitely wanted to see photos of the kids of a hardworking mongoose who had just freed her from a dungeon.

Gogo began opening the lockets that hung around her neck one by one. "Here's Mango," she said, giving the photo inside the locket a little kiss, then closing it again. "This one is Tango," she said, opening another locket. "Here's Argo and Ergo, oh, and this is such a cute one of Oswego." Downer came to look as well. "Here's Django. And Bingo. And Dingo." Each young mongoose was as magically adorable as the next. "Durango. Manchego. Logo, Togo, and Pogo. Right after their haircuts, you see? Fandango, Quetzaltenango, Ego." She paused a moment. "And my youngest: Bob."

"Children are the Best Thing in the World," Downer said. Gogo nodded.

What a kind world she had wandered into, Fred was thinking. A world where you were saved from a dungeon by a creature who didn't even know you. Maybe her mom had walked through that lantern because somehow she knew that it led to a world where you could expect such kindness from strangers—

"Well, enough of the picture gallery," Gogo said. "Cash or credit, my new friends?"

Fred looked over at Downer, who gave an elephantish shrug.

Gogo laughed, then clarified. "Oh, I don't mean for seeing photos of my kids. That would be absurd! I mean for the dungeon liberation. Cash or credit?"

A colder breeze passed through the valley, bending the heads of the wildflowers.

Gogo added, "I can waive the 3% surcharge on cards, if that helps?" She fidgeted with a flier she held in one hand.

"I don't have cash *or* credit," offered Fred. "I'm actually in my pajamas."

"I am also without either," Downer added, hanging his head.

"Oh man, not again," Gogo said, despondently. "This is more frustrating than being mistaken for a meerkat. More maddening than Jell-O that never sets." She started pacing. From her back pocket she unfolded a flier identical to the one pasted on the dungeon's interior wall:

She explained that she had received an anonymous tip that the young deer was in this dungeon. The cryptic letter had made it seem that the dungeon would be a sure thing.

"So you weren't sent here by the Rat Queen?" Fred asked, chewing her nails in thought.

"Not directly. Though I did come in search of the deer on account of the Rat's flier."

"That still counts as the Rat saving us," Downer said to Fred, in his devotion.

Gogo sneezed louder than you might expect from a small creature. "Sorry, I sneeze when I'm anxious." She sneezed again. "I'm just under a lot of pressure right now." She was interrupted by her own sneezing—albeit politely, into her elbow—and then she took off her backpack and started digging through it, while she mumbled: "Phooey on that ridiculous Rule 79; it's been a catastrophe, and I have so many sweeties depending on me, and they don't ask for much, but—" Finally Gogo found what she wanted from her backpack. It wasn't A Good Night's Sleep. Nor was it Knowing That You Are Loved. Or even a handkerchief. But she did pull out the object like it was some kind of Solution.

It was a jar of pickles.

"Helps calm me down," Gogo said, gesturing with the pickle between crunches. "Great pickles." Pre-sneeze face, but then no sneeze. "Not too sour." A breath in, but again no sneeze. "Where were we then? Want one?"

Fred smiled, which surprised her. She looked over at Downer, and then back at Gogo. "Is that a real pickle?" she asked.

"Of course it's a real pickle," Gogo said. "You think it's a maraschino cherry?"

Downer smiled, too. It was as if the pickles had been made out of Fred and Downer's bickering.

Gogo said, "I know I'll come up with something, I just have to think." What our friends didn't know but might have guessed was that Gogo had gotten out of pickles before. Before Rat Rule 79, Gogo had been working as an entertainer at . . . those parties that used to be thrown for children until they were forbidden from even being mentioned. Gogo managed to keep things together then, and she would do so again, she was sure of it. Sort of. She paused. "Hey, did you guys ever hear the one about how the cucumber became a pickle?"

Fred and Downer shook their heads.

"She went through a jarring experience," said Gogo, and added her own smile.

Nine Dots and Four Lines

Fred's planet pajamas were not just any pajamas. These pajamas had pockets. When Gogo had asked for cash or credit, Fred had checked her pockets. You never know. She didn't find money there. But she did find a soft, old piece of paper. As soon as she felt it, she knew what it was. It came from a different evening of eating takeout lo mein noodles with her mom, months earlier. The night when her mom had first announced the latest move. Fred knew her mom was a math professor, and her mom had more than once said to her that when you're a professor, you spend a good portion of your life being sent from town to town to town— that was the way it was. Fred didn't want to hurt her mom's feelings, but she wanted to tell her that maybe she wasn't so good, then, at what she did. Instead, Fred said that she was bored. She didn't say anything about the move, but instead complained that their life had become really, really boring.

"I get it," her mom said. (Which usually meant she didn't.) Then her mom said that you never have to be bored so long as you have paper and a pen.

Fred had a number of differences of opinion with this statement. She expressed them quite strongly. One might even say that she yelled. But I won't say that. It was Fred's wholly reasonable opinion that, yes, you could be bored, even if you had a paper and pen.

Anyhow, her mom seemed not to notice Fred's dissent. Her mom drew nine dots on a piece of paper like so:

She told Fred that you had to find a way to connect all nine dots with just four lines, and without picking up your pen. This was a puzzle that she, Fred's mom, had liked when she herself was a little girl, and her own mom—Fred's Oma—had shown it to her. It was a very ancient puzzle, but still a fresh one. It was a puzzle that never got old.

Time is a funny thing, even if it isn't an illusion. Or even if it is. Fred didn't take an interest in the puzzle at the time, or at least no more than a brief moment of interest during which she pretended *not* to take an interest but hoped the answer would leap out at her immediately so she could offer it casually and impress her mom, who didn't understand, Fred thought, how little she knew about her own daughter. Fred wanted to impress her mom the way that it's impressive when someone pulls a quarter out of your ear, even for the fifteenth time. But I'll tell you now, because suspense can be annoying, that Fred didn't solve the puzzle. She put the piece of paper in her pocket. Then time passed. And though Fred was not perceptibly different, she became interested in the puzzle again. At school, when she was feeling betwixt and between, she would pull out the puzzle and spend some time with it. It was a curiously companionable feeling, to have a problem that she couldn't quite solve, but which she assumed was not impossible.

Chapter Thought

"I have to head off to the Bag again very soon," said Downer, finishing off a pickle. "It's only fair that I try again to let the Rat out of the Bag given that she got me out of the dungeon—"

"But *Gogo* let you out of the dungeon," Fred pointed out again. "First off, we should help—"

Gogo said, "Oh, don't worry about me. That's what I get for following unsigned tips." She shrugged, but it wasn't convincing.

Clouds were covering up the sunlight, lending a thoughtful color to the grasses.

"The girl isn't wrong," Downer said to Gogo. "We owe you. All of us do: me, Fred, and the Rat Queen too. You took the trouble to say Knock, Knock, and it's our obligation to say Who's There, if you know what I mean. We'll help you. I just don't know how yet." Downer took a seat to show his solidarity.

Do you like pickles? Pickles are so much more than a surprisingly delicious companion to a peanut butter sandwich. Pickles are long-lasting and nutritious. It is not for no reason that pregnant women are known to crave pickles. You might even say that each of us began life nurtured on pickles, and that the story we make of our lives is the particular way we solve our own personal pickles. Or you might not say that. Fred, Downer, and Gogo each took another pickle from the jar.

"I've got it," Fred said. "Very simple. Gogo should go to the Bag with you, Downer. I realize the Rat's not free, but she's obviously still putting out fliers, sending out letters, still getting things done. She owes Gogo for letting *you* out. She would help, right?"

"Of course she would," Downer said. "She's the Rat of Rightness and Reasoning and Ready-to-Boil Rice and—"

Gogo waved a paw dismissively. "I'm sure the Rat has enough on her mind. I doubt I'm one of her favorites, after all the complaints my kids made about No One Can Disagree with Rat Rule 79. I can go back to fighting cobras, it's reliable work—"

"That's crazy," Downer said, standing. "I insist. You can ride on my back if that makes it easier. The only problem is if you're too afraid of Ferlings. I imagine the Rat is totally surrounded by Ferlings; otherwise she'd be able to get out of the Bag on her own."

"I've never seen a Ferling," Gogo admitted. "But I doubt they could be as frightening as cobras with convictions."

"You should do it," Fred said encouragingly.

Gogo gave her lockets another tender look.

"You won't be alone, Gogo," Downer added. There'll be an elephant in the room with you."

"Do you think she'll mistake me for a meerkat? No disrespect to meerkats. But I really don't need another setback. And I hear she's quite strange these days."

"There's no way she'll think you're a meerkat," Downer said. "She knows everything there is to know and more."

Gogo folded up the WANTED flier and returned it to her back pocket. "Okay. I'm in." Another breeze passed through the field, so that it seemed like the flowers were nodding their approval. Or trembling with worry. "You're coming with us, Fred, right?"

"I need to wait right here for my mother," Fred declared. She stated her plan like she was saying the sky was blue. It was an immovable fact. She'd already traveled to a new town, with weird fortune cookies, and then through a lantern; the last thing she needed was to move again, further from where she had last seen her mom, to visit a power-crazed, birthday-hating Rat who was, apparently, stuck in a Bag. The Rat owed Gogo. The Rat owed Downer. But the Rat owed Fred nothing. To the Rat, Fred was Nobody, and she knew it.

"Is it that you're fed up with me?" Downer asked.

"No, it's not that," Fred said, irritated.

Gogo offered: "You want to have these pickles to keep with you?" She held out the jar sincerely.

"Thanks, but I'm all right," Fred said bravely. "I'm only really into pickles if there's peanut butter and bread to go with them."

"I understand," Gogo said. "Peanut butter is illegal under Rat Rule 79, but it's not a clause that's much enforced. I just mention it." Gogo gave her a hug.

Downer added, "Don't worry too much about being completely, totally, utterly alone in this land. Don't worry about not really understanding the rules here, or the geography, or anything else. And don't worry that no one loves me. You're in the land where Children are, officially, The Best Thing in the World. What can go wrong?"

"Um, yeah, what he said," said Gogo, climbing onto Downer's back. She opened up a map, and they headed away.

Chapter Dot,
Dot, Dot

Fred reached deeper in her pocket and found another piece of paper. It was a different game her mom had once shown her. But also with dots.

They had been sitting at a donut shop in Boulder, Colorado. Fred had ordered a donut with pink frosting and sprinkles. It was a donut shop in a mall that also had a dentists' office, and they were at the donut shop waiting for the dentist appointment, with one of those buzzers that lit up when it was your turn. What kind of mom took you out for donuts before the dentist? Her mom. In some ways her mom was like a kid.

Which reminded Fred that, at some point, her mom really was a kid. It was dizzying to think of your mom existing before you were born. It seemed wrong. Or at least incorrect.

At the donut shop, Fred said she was afraid of the dentist. Or perhaps it had been on her face. And afraid may not have been quite the right word. Her mom turned over the tray liner and said, "Let's play a game." She pulled out a marker pen, handed it to Fred, and asked her to draw a squiggle.

"What do you mean, a squiggle?"

"Any kind of squiggle. A random squiggle."

Fred drew a loopity-looping-zig-zagger of a squiggle.

"Alrighty then." Her mom rotated the tray liner paper. She looked at the squiggle seriously. She rotated it again. With respect. "Very interesting. Yes, very, very interesting," she said as if she were reading a fortune. Finally, she drew one large dark dot. "That's its eye," Fred's mom said. "The monster's eye."

And there was the monster. A cute little monster. A reluctant fire-breathing monster, it seemed.

"Now I'll do a squiggle and you choose where the eye will go," her mom said.

They went back and forth like this. Again and again, the nothings in particular became somethings in particular. Often they became sea life. Or close-ups of the tiny creatures Fred had been told lived in volcanoes, or ponds. Occasionally a land monster turned up. Or a creature with wings, or something narrow and burrowing. A whole silly menagerie, all of whom felt like friends.

Fred remembered thumbing the fallen sprinkles from the corner of the plastic tray. And her mom saying, "It's weird, right, how much power a little dot can have." Eventually the dentist buzzer must have rung, she must have faced the dentist, but that part—she didn't really remember.

Chapter Second Thoughts

Marking time is illegal under Rat Rule 79. But if I were to describe how long Fred sat there, outside the dungeon/toolshed, thinking what to do next, I would say the amount of time felt about equivalent to being at the supermarket's deli counter with her mom, waiting for their number to turn up on the Now Serving screen, and then asking for a half a pound of thinly sliced—very thinly, please—Muenster cheese, and after the number was called and the order was taken, the additional forever it took for the wrapped cheese to be delivered to her mother's hand. Which, by standard clock time, let's guesstimate, is probably about eight minutes.

That was about how long it took Fred to realize that she *did* want to go with Downer and Gogo to see the Ratty Rat Rat of Rationality and Reason and Ribbed T-Shirts and Cures for Ringworm and so on. What made her think her mom would turn up in the middle of this field? Or even that the sky was really blue. Wasn't that a trick of optics? The sad truth was she had no idea where the lantern had sent her mom. And the Rat had a reputation for knowing things. The Rat might know where her mom had gone. Maybe? Surely? Fred could still make out Downer and Gogo in the distance. She ran across the field as quickly as she could to catch up with them.

But then when she did catch up, she was embarrassed to admit that she thought, or at least hoped, that the Rat could help her too. Gasping for breath but trying to be casual, Fred said, "There was . . . something . . . I forgot to ask."

"You look fatigued as a featherless chicken," Gogo said. "Breathless as a bill-less duck."

Fred panted: "Have you seen a woman, like a human one, dressed sort of like she's going to, like, some sort of party?"

Gogo and Downer both looked alarmed.

Very alarmed.

Very, very alarmed.

Which seemed weird to Fred. Was her mom okay?

"Fred, you don't mean, umm, a B.P., do you?" Downer asked in a whisper.

"A B.P.?" Fred said in a normal voice.

"You know," Gogo said very quietly. Then she sneezed. "A B. *party.*"

In a still normal voice, which seemed loud after the whispers, Fred said, "A birthday party?" She had not taken Rat Rule 79 very seriously, as you may recall, and had already forgotten its final bold-faced clause. Downer and Gogo grimaced and hopped around, looking this way and that, as if expecting spies or sirens. "I don't think so," Fred went on, unembarrassed. "More like a grown-up party. Just one of those boring get-togethers where everybody talks about the most boring things in the world."

"So not a B.P.?" Downer asked.

"I don't think so," Fred said.

"Ah okay, thank goodness," Gogo said. "I feel more relieved than a half-starved ring-tailed lemur in the produce aisle." She was clutching her lockets again. "So long as it's not a B.P., then we are A-OK."

Downer said, "Yep, a B.P. would be a catastrophe. Though P.B.—that we could get away with. Peanut Butter is frowned upon, for reasons I really don't understand, but, like Gogo said earlier, it's not an absolute no-no. . . ."

Fred said, "Those rules are silly, everyone loves birthd—"

Gogo said, "Shush!" and Downer said "Hush!"—both with goggle-eyed intensity.

You may remember that only a short time earlier Fred had been against a very particular B.P.—her own. But in the face of confusing and random opposition, she was beginning to feel very pro-birthday parties, at least as a general concept. "As it happens, tomorrow is *my* birthda—"

Gogo jumped on Fred's back and covered Fred's mouth with her paws. Downer unfurled and held before Fred's nose his copy of THE ESSENTIAL AND VERY GOOD AND NO ONE CAN DISAGREE WITH RAT RULE 79.

It was all done with a great deal of decisiveness, of conviction. Though Fred was not impressed. Shaking the mongoose off of her, she said, "So not only can I not *have* a . . . B.P., but I can't even say B.P.?"

Gogo and Downer nodded. Gogo pointed at the relevant passage of the flier like a schoolteacher, and not a great one.

Fred went on: "So basically a B.P. is, like . . . the elephant in the room?"

"Are you loyal to the Rat, or is your fealty to the Fearsome Ferlings?" Downer demanded. "Out with it!"

"I don't care one way or the other about the Rat *or* the Fearsome Ferlings, whatever they are, whoever she is," Fred said, raising her voice. "I'm trying to find my mom, that's it. But you can't just set a rule that people can't get older. You can't set a rule that grass can't be green. Or that sugar makes you strong. It's not that I agree or disagree with Rat Rule 79. It's that not getting older is an impossible task."

Downer blinked his eyes sadly. Gogo advanced a few cautious steps and gently held out her map to Fred. "I'm sorry, I thought you knew," Gogo said. "The rule *is* Impossible. This is the Land of Impossibility."

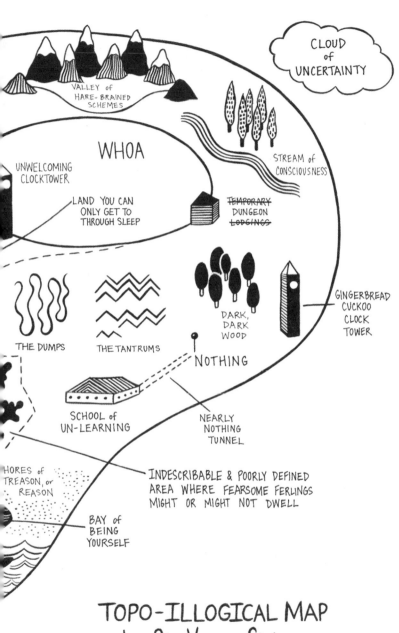

CLOUD of UNCERTAINTY

VALLEY of HARE-BRAINED SCHEMES

WHOA

UNWELCOMING CLOCKTOWER

STREAM of CONSCIOUSNESS

LAND YOU CAN ONLY GET TO THROUGH SLEEP

~~TEMPORARY~~ DUNGEON ~~LODGINGS~~

THE DUMPS

THE TANTRUMS

DARK, DARK WOOD

GINGERBREAD CUCKOO CLOCK TOWER

NOTHING

SCHOOL of UN-LEARNING

NEARLY NOTHING TUNNEL

HORES of TREASON, or REASON

INDESCRIBABLE & POORLY DEFINED AREA WHERE FEARSOME FERLINGS MIGHT OR MIGHT NOT DWELL

BAY of BEING YOURSELF

TOPO-ILLOGICAL MAP
by Sir Vayer Sirius

Chapter Fork

If you want to know how much steel a
  wooden ship can carry,
Or what would happen to a parakeet in outer space,
If you want to know how hot it would need to be
  for a friend named Larry
to burst into flames—

This was the curiously cheerful song Downer sang as the trio made their way across the field. Fred had been convinced that if anyone could help her find her mom, the Rat could. Gogo consulted her topo-illogical map of The Land of Impossibility. The map looked less than new, and Fred noticed a few disconcerting labels on it like, "No One Really Is Sure About This Part" and "Whoa, Baby." As they progressed, following Gogo's directions, the field sloped uphill. The density of rocks increased.

Downer's song began to change:

If you want to know how cacti grow
Or where the underground rivers flow
If your ice won't melt
And your breakfast is spelt—

Eventually they arrived at a stream bordered by trembling poplar trees. The poplars had tall, thin, whitish trunks, with leaves that alternated between silvery and swimming pool. As the wind blew, you could make out the sound of the papery leaves moving against one another.

On one of the trees hung a large sign that read:

THIS WAY→

and below that

←THAT WAY

"Which way?" Fred asked.

"To be honest as a puppy, I can't tell," said Gogo. "I'm as tuckered out as the tiniest sleigh dog. Let's figure it out after a little stream-time."

Gogo set her backpack down on the shore, then dove in, rolling around and over and figure-eighting in the river. Downer sucked the water up in his trunk, then sprayed it into his mouth in happy gulps. Fred scooped up water with her hands. It tasted cold and delicious. All water is supposedly made of the same stuff—water—but the taste of water is never the same. In Colorado, Fred had noticed the water tasted a tiny bit like licking a nickel. In Kansas, ever so slightly like soap. Anyhow, this water, wherever it was from, tasted especially good. How peaceful she felt.

But as Fred reached into the water for another scoop, she got a funny feeling: the feeling of being watched.

The Know-It-Owl

A bove Fred, partly camouflaged by the white bark of the poplars, was a stout and stately owl, mostly white but with checks of dark brown. The owl was perched atop the **THIS WAY→** sign. Its dark pupils were circled by orange irises. Its beak appeared to be that of a creature capable of eating another creature's eyeball without being too troubled.

Well, reader, this wasn't just any owl. It was a Know-It-Owl.

Fred didn't like being watched. As her friends played in the water, Fred addressed the owl: "Excuse me, but do you know which of these paths go to the Rat?"

The Know-It-Owl blinked, but said nothing.

Fred stood up straight and spoke again. "Hello there Mister, or Missus, Owl. You look like you know your way around here." Having moved around so much, Fred had a soft spot in her heart for awkward newcomers. She had a gentle way with them. "That's why I asked: Do you know which of these paths goes to the Rat?"

The Know-It-Owl blinked again. Then said, in a not particularly friendly voice: "These paths stay right where they are. Neither of them *goes* anywhere."

Gogo was now watching the conversation between the girl and the bird of prey.

Fred politely said, "Oh yes, sure, excuse me. What I mean is: Which of these paths can we take to the Rat?"

Readjusting her wings, the Know-It-Owl let out what sounded like a sigh. "Take something that doesn't belong to you? That's not right. Not right at all."

Gogo was now at Fred's side, with her paws up in a fighting stance. What you may or may not know about mongeese is that they are famously brave fighters, as small as they are. "All right, Menacing Beak Bird, you know very well what the child is asking. She asked very politely! And may I remind you that Children are the Greatest Thing in the World. Answer the child's question as to whether we can walk down one of these paths to get to the Rat, or else!"

The Know-It-Owl gave an owlish version of a shrug. "What do I know about your walking abilities?"

"Do you or don't you know the way to the Rat?" Fred asked.

"Yes," said the Know-It-Owl.

"This birdbrain doesn't know anything," Gogo said.

"I know where I am," the Know-It-Owl said. "Which is more than you can say for yourself."

"It's a fork in the road," Fred said, trying to bring the conversation back to the question of which way to go.

"If I saw a fork in the road, I would pick it up," the owl said.

"Let's forget about this polly-wants-a-cracker," Gogo said, pulling at Fred's hand. "She's more slippery than an eel, more needlesome than a needlefish, more—"

The Know-It-Owl spread her wings out fully. It must be said, they were magnificent wings. Broader than you might have expected. Owls are swift, strong predators. And mongoose, it is said, is very tasty (though I promise I have never eaten one). Downer came and picked up Gogo with his trunk. "Let's calm down, Gogo"—Gogo was still muttering insults at the owl—"this owl doesn't like us, but that's okay, we don't need to be liked, and it's not her job to like us . . . ."

The Know-It-Owl's wings were still threateningly outstretched—or was she only airing them out?

Fred sort of liked the owl, and the owl's bizarrely straightforward answers. The pattern of the owl's feathers reminded Fred of a red and white check tablecloth. "For some reason, you remind me of a unicorn," Fred whispered to the owl. "Not that I believe in unicorns. But I mean, in how surprising and beautiful you are. A rare creature in the woods." Fred shrugged. "Just sharing a thought."

The Know-It-Owl folded back her wings and made no comment as to whether or not unicorns exist, or whether she was beautiful and surprising or not, or whether it was or wasn't her job to like these three lost travelers, or whether it was their job to like her.

"Who are you, anyway?" Fred asked the Know-It-Owl. "You look . . . familiar."

"I'm Somebody," the Know-It-Owl said.

"Same as me," said Downer. "Though I've been known to be confused with Nobody."

The Know-It-Owl looked left and right, as if preparing to leave.

"We still don't know which way to go," Fred said, looking at the owl.

The Know-It-Owl ceased fidgeting and returned Fred's steady gaze. "You say this is a fork in the road?"

Fred nodded.

"I say it's a spoon." At that, the owl spread her wings again, but this time flew away.

Chapter Spoon

"Oh sure, maybe it's a ladle," Gogo said with annoyance. "I'm so wise, I'm like, Maybe it's a pizza cutter. Maybe it's not a fork in the road, it's a butter knife. It's a potato peeler."

"Yeah, what the owl said, it's kind of like a weird fortune cookie," Fred said, trying to make Gogo feel better. She could see that something about that owl had really gotten to Gogo. Maybe that owls hunt small, cute mammals.

"Maybe it's a tool for shelling peanuts," Downer offered seriously.

"You don't get it, Downer," Gogo said. "It's nonsense. There is no spoon."

Fred said, "What if she means what she says?"

Gogo shook her head and rolled her eyes.

"Okay, pickle-eater," Fred said with a laugh. "I'm just saying that all her answers to our questions—she never lied. She was just extreme about responding to what we said instead of to what we meant."

"I'm not seeing a teaspoon, a tablespoon or a soup spoon," Downer said, doing a careful survey of the ground. "I'm not seeing a grapefruit spoon. I'm not even seeing a ladle."

Fred walked among the poplars, beyond the **THIS WAY→/ ←THAT WAY** signs. "I get it!" she called out. "The owl means what the owl says. I know where to go!"

WE (AND ONLY WE!) WILL SAVE THE RAT!

Future Liberators of the Rat
Gather Here!

ABANDON ALL HOPE NON-LOVERS OF THE RAT.

Welcome,
Rescuers of the Rat!

Workin'
Hard

The Set of All Sets
That Aren't Your Set

Dear reader, if you think that you'll probably meet that troublesome Know-It-Owl again, you're right. But for now let's not worry about it. And if you think that Fred really did solve the spoon riddle the owl gave her, then you're also right. And if you thought she didn't: that's okay too, since being wrong is also a good habit. But the fork in the road really was a spoon—that was what Fred realized, which is to say that if you followed **THIS WAY** you would find that it met up with **THAT WAY**, and vice versa, like the round sides of a spoon meeting up at the tip; the two paths followed their own arcs out and then came back together. It was as if our friends couldn't go wrong. Or could only go wrong. Either way, they were again on their way to see the Ratty Rat Rat of Rationality and Radiation Therapy and Rimless Sunglasses and so on.

Soon they reached a high plain surrounded by mountains on three sides. Crowded in that plain were creatures of many sizes and colors, but mostly rabbits. Some were Flemish giant rabbits. Some hares. Some bunnies. And some were Patagonian maras, which look like giant rabbits with a bit of rattishness to them. I mean rattishness in the best way. A large banner in the middle of the field read:

WELCOME, RESCUERS OF THE RAT!

Another nearby read:

FUTURE LIBERATORS OF THE RAT GATHER HERE!

Another:

ABANDON ALL HOPE NON-LOVERS OF THE RAT!

Then higher and larger than the other banners:

WE (AND ONLY WE!) WILL SAVE THE RAT!

A dozen Arctic hares huddled near canvas tents. A smaller group of desert cottontails looked to be doing some sort of project with popsicle sticks and squares of yellow paper. Nearby, a tall, jack-eared rabbit was pacing and counting at the perimeter of what looked to be a life-sized version of a game of checkers. Further along, several large maps, each in different colors, were unfolded like giant picnic blankets. Here a group of fuzzy lop-eareds was making a list. Another group was sitting neatly at a table and folding up dough into fortune cookies. A group of rabbits is sometimes called a fluffle, and this field of fluffles appeared to be up to something substantial.

One pale large-eared creature appeared to be marking out sight lines with a compass. A distant crowd of bunnies were wearing green or yellow jerseys, as if for a game of soccer.

Many clues suggested that our friends were in the totally, absolutely, very right place to be in their quest for the Rat, but other hard-to-describe feelings argued that they were in the totally, absolutely, very wrong place.

Fred, Downer, and Gogo moved among the furry army that mysteriously took no note of them. A tall grey-eared rabbit in overalls, speaking into what looked like a headset, was walking upright, straight toward Gogo, while dictating, "Two apples, midsize. Three celery sticks, with leaves. Thirteen wrenches. . . . Oh, hello!" the headsetted rabbit said cheerily. Perhaps too cheerily. "Can I help you find your team?"

"Um . . . team?" said Fred.

The rabbit abruptly muttered into his headset microphone, "Let's try not to split hares." He turned back to Fred and company. "No need to be shy. You must be on *some* team. We welcome non-rabbits! Nice slippers, by the way. Very nice. Are you a child? We love children. As the Rat says—and we love the Rat!—Children Are the Best Thing in the World."

"Oh, thanks," Fred said uneasily. She had forgotten she still had those bunny—or were they rabbit?—slippers on. Fred turned to Downer and Gogo, who offered only a shrug and an eye roll, respectively. "If we *are* on a team," Fred guessed, "then we don't know it."

"Ah, I understand," the rabbit said, reaching into the back pocket of his overalls and pulling out a flip wallet that displayed a golden circle. "Don't worry. You can tell me. I'm credentialed. Are you guys here on the Espionage and Escalation team?"

"Oh, no!" Fred said. "Definitely not."

"Counterespionage and De-Escalation team?"

"It's possible we're just lost," Gogo said.

"Or unwanted," Downer suggested. "And we would be totally fine with that."

"That's impossible," the rabbit said. "If you are Rescuers of the Rat, you're definitely on a team. And if you aren't Rescuers of the Rat, you wouldn't be here. We account for everything, for everyone. Give me a minute." The rabbit looked over pages in a notebook. "What do you remember about your team?" the rabbit persisted. "Anything at all?"

"We were never on a team," Fred admitted.

"No one would want me on their team," added Downer.

"And my availability is limited," Gogo said, caressing her lockets that held the photos of her children.

The rabbit mumbled to himself. "Let's see. . . . We have openings on the Cheerers, the Faithful Documenters, the Turncoat Saboteurs, the Dislikers of Tuna—"

"Who?"

"—the Under-wearers, the False Pallbearers . . . my goodness, it *is* overwhelming when I realize how much there is to do before we can rescue the Rat—"

Fred interrupted: "Maybe we're a team, the three of us, but we didn't know we were a team. We're the team that is trying to go talk directly to the Rat—"

"—who is still in the Bag," Downer said.

"—but who accepts visitors," Gogo said.

"—we hope," added Fred.

"Interesting, yes," said the rabbit. "We know all about the Bag. We have been Rescuers of the Rat for generations and generations. Even before she needed rescuers. Even before she was born. I'm actually, just a moment—"

Seemingly from nowhere the rabbit pulled out an accordion and started to sing a ditty that in some ways was like Downer's and in some ways not. Three smaller bunnies emerged to do a line dance in the background as the head-setted rabbit sang:

> *Before Ratty-Rat*
> *there never was a Rat*
> *or a this or a that*
> *and who were we then?*
> *Before Ratty-Rat*
> *At the laundromat*
> *With a half-pickled pickle*
> *And a spell that was fickle*
> *And no thermostat*
> *Now what do you think of that?*
> *Now what do you think of that?*
> *We are coming to save you,*
> *Save you, save you*
> *Ratty Rat!*
> *As soon as we are ready.*

The backup bunnies dispersed. The headsetted rabbit put away the small accordion, spun three times in a circle, and took a little bow.

Splitting Hares

Downer didn't like the rabbit's Ratty Rat song so much, to be honest.

And Gogo was growing impatient. "I don't want to start a fight here, but I have a burrow full of hungry little mongeese—there's Mango, Django, Manchego, there's Ergo, Argo and Bingo, and, well I'm not going to through them all—but I'm saying we are the team that's looking for the Rat *today*. Not the team that's making plans to look for the Rat in some mythical tomorrow. If you haven't got any advice for a team like that, we'll be on our way—"

"No such team," said the rabbit. "No team going today. Absolutely not." The mountains surrounding the high plain seemed to hem them in as the words were spoken.

"No such team?"

"We're not today creatures. We're tomorrow creatures. So is the rat. Tomorrow is always a better day. No today teams."

"You've been working for all these years," Gogo persisted, "and with all these rabbits, but do you have a plan for when you will go to, you know, liberate her?"

"We *do* have space on the calendar-maker team. Though of course their work needs to be verified by the triangulators. And if you want—"

Downer interrupted with his calmly depressing voice. "We're not wanted. We're fine with that."

To which Gogo, who Fred noticed was now eating another pickle, added: "We're on no team. We're just passing through."

The rabbit tilted his head. "So you're not Rescuers of the Rat?"

"I guess not," Fred said. "Not in the way you must mean."

"So you're not with us?"

"No, we're not."

"Then you must be against us."

"We're not!"

"You're with us?"

"I'm confused,"

"It's very clear," the rabbit said. "Those who are not with us must abandon all hope. Okay, I'm marking it down now. I'll call up the team that attends to our Enemies. Please wait here."

Not the 91st Chapter

Something I like about rabbits is that they can jump thirteen times the length of their bodies. That's like a normal kid jumping across a four-lane highway and then some. I know this because Fred's old neighbor used to raise rabbits. Specifically, angora rabbits. Have you seen angora rabbits? They look like tumbleweed-sized cotton balls. Fred's neighbor fed his angora rabbits papayas. (That was one of the weirder neighbors, in a charming way; there were perks to moving around, it wasn't all lonely birthdays.) Papayas smell like old socks, it's true. But they are also tasty. At least to rabbits. Angora rabbits, in cleaning themselves with their tongues, swallow so much of their own wool that the wool accumulates in hard lumps in their intestinal tracts, allowing nothing else to pass. This is, as you might imagine, unpleasant. It's also lethal. Papayas somehow remedy this. Years ago, when I told this to Fred, she told me that what I was saying wasn't true. She used to be like that: what she didn't like, she deemed "not true." She didn't like these facts about angora rabbits. Therefore they were impossible, according to her. I was thinking about this now, how the rabbits were like their own wool clogging up the tunnels of their own warrens, which is another less than appealing image, but these rabbits really irritate me, even with their inevitably good hearts and impressive engineering skills.

And now these rabbits thought our friends were their enemies.

While Gogo was arguing with the headsetted rabbit about whether they were or weren't enemies, Downer and Fred hung back. "Their hoptimism is maddening," sighed Downer.

"Hoptimism?" asked Fred.

"They've got about as much chance of reaching the Rat as two locked boxes, each containing each other's key, have a chance of being opened."

"Where did you hear that?"

"Hear what?"

"Did you make that up, about the two locked boxes? That was in my last fortune cookie."

"I heard it from you," said Downer. He sighed again and patted at the ground with his heavy foot. "I feel bad for those rabbits. All that planning comes from never wanting to be wrong. If you're terrified of making a mistake, then you never try. Instead you make plans for trying. Look at me: I failed. But big deal, I'll try again. I'm very comfortable failing."

Fred said, "Yeah, I'm not surprised these rabbits are still hanging out on this field of nothing but dreams."

"You used to be so easily surprised," Downer said, nudging Fred gently with his trunk.

Gogo's argument with the headsetted rabbit was growing more animated.

Fred said, "Ha ha, I'm getting older and wiser—"

"—Oh, man—"

"I'll be ninety-one—"

"—please stop—"

"—before these guys have even spelled RA—"

"—now we're in for it—"

The atmosphere around Fred was changing dramatically. As if birds were suddenly taking flight, glaciers were crashing into the sea, the sea was rising, the grass at their feet was growing monstrously fast, and children everywhere were graduating.

The headsetted rabbit hopped over to Fred. "Repeat what you said?"

"I don't want to hurt any bunny's feelings—"

The rabbit persisted: "Could you say what you said again, please? For the record." The rabbit was holding what looked to be a small recording device in one paw.

"I just said I was getting . . . older and wis—"

"She said no such thing," Gogo interrupted, inserting herself between Fred and the rabbit. "She's lying like a ferret feigning indifference to scrambled eggs. Like a bear claiming to be awake all winter."

"She's new here," Downer pleaded.

Ignoring them, the rabbit pushed the recording device closer to Fred, forcing Fred back a step. "And *how* do you plan to get older and wiser?" pressed the rabbit.

"The things kids say these days," Downer interjected, faking a chortling laugh and covering up Fred's mouth with his trunk.

To which Gogo added: "Ha, ha, Children *Are* the Best Thing in the World, but they say the darnedest—"

"Excuse me," said the rabbit firmly. "Let the girl speak for herself. Okay. How *exactly* do you plan to get older and wiser?"

Dear reader, do you know about that kind of quiet that can happen even as a waterfall is rushing, or a wind is blowing? The quiet of sitting in a moving train, say, when you think you can hear your hair growing, or your skin shedding layers? It's noisy and quiet at the same time, and your mind makes a whirring sound as it fails to come up with a thought? That was the kind of loud quiet that Fred heard as the rabbit's recording device awaited her response. Fred found herself thinking about her birthday, one day away—or was it already here?—and the birthday party that wasn't going to happen, because she had just moved to a new town and didn't really know anybody. Unless somehow Downer and Gogo were "in" her town, which it seemed like they weren't. And there was her mom, but adults don't count. And her mom wasn't even here! But that was all okay, she would pass her birthday imagining that everywhere she went she was being celebrated *in secret*. The celebration was a secret she could detect only through, say, a glance, a dropped coin, an unusual fortune cookie. All clues. Maybe even a cute, shy boy would enigmatically leave behind a scrap of paper, with a doodle on it, intended to win her attention. Because someone, somewhere, surely, was pleased that another year had passed, another inch had been grown, and—

"Excuse me," the rabbit prompted. "I was asking: *How* do you plan to get older and wiser?"

To which Fred found herself saying, "*In the usual ways. I'm going to have a birthday.*" Fred could tell that what she was saying was shocking and disturbing to everyone around her—so she said it some more. "And then another birthday and another birthday and another birthday and another—"

Too Many Birthdays
Can Kill You

The sky darkened. The headsetted rabbit hopped into a nearby hole in the ground and vanished. Teams in various colored jerseys were running this way and that, diving into other holes, huddling behind large rocks. All that panicked hopping and running produced a sound like the drumming of an approaching army of chaos, or an oncoming storm. Soon the only creatures in sight were our three friends, huddled together, kept company only by the now unattended banners: **WELCOME, RESCUERS OF THE RAT! FUTURE LIBERATORS OF THE RAT GATHER HERE! ABANDON ALL HOPE NON-LOVERS OF THE RAT.** And: **WE (AND ONLY WE!) WILL SAVE THE RAT!**

The feeling was of something enormous approaching. As Fred stood there—some might say Fred was quivering with fear, but I won't say that—she thought she spied a giant yeti in the distance; then she thought what she saw was closer to the size of a grizzly bear; nope, was it a large hound? Normally things grow larger as they get closer, but this approaching creature was doing the opposite.

The creature was a cuddly little dog, maybe part Shih Tzu. The little dog was yapping: "Birthday violation! Birthday violation! On order of the Rat! Disperse! Disperse!"

Yet who was there to disperse? Only Fred and her friends remained.

You may have noticed by now Fred's tendency to get lost in her own thoughts. While the dog was yapping, Fred was thinking about how she had once been told that Shih Tzus had been bred to fit in emperors' sleeves to keep them warm and company. And then she was thinking about how she had been told that that kind of phrase—*to keep them warm and company,* or, say, *he opened the door and my heart*—was called a *zeugma.* And perhaps one reason she was thinking of the very odd word **zeugma** was because the dog was wearing a large tag that read: **DOGMA**. Fred couldn't remember quite what dogma meant, but it sounded cute.

Gogo sneezed. She nervously caressed the lockets that held the photos of her children. Then she sneezed again.

"I know a guilty sneeze when I hear it," Dogma woofed. "Hand over the candles."

"We've got no candles, Dogma," Downer said glumly.

"Hand over the cake," Dogma said.

"You think we can afford cake?" Gogo said, then sneezed yet again.

Dogma sniffed at the air. "I don't smell cake. I'll give you that. But the girl said the B word four times and implied another four-score more. She pronounced plans for getting older and wiser *in the usual ways.* She—"

"Look at her, Dogma. Does she *look* like she's getting older and wiser?"

As you may remember, Fred was still wearing fluffy bunny

84

slippers and planet pajamas. May she always wear fluffy bunny slippers and planet pajamas, if she wants to.

"And, as you must acknowledge, Children are the Greatest Thing in the World. She is clearly a child and has every intention of remaining a child—"

As these questionable defenses were being offered, Fred folded her arms and thought impatiently about peanut butter and pickle sandwiches.

Sometimes it's good to have no idea of the perils of your situation.

"Regardless of candle or cake possession, the girl, who may or may not be a child, spoke of plans to get older, she spoke of the B word. These are undeniable violations of Rat Rule 79."

Gogo blew her nose, then managed: "A violation of the letter of the law but not the spirit of the law, right?"

"The spirit?" Dogma said. "I don't believe in spirits. And neither does the Rat Queen, who is entirely rational and good and righteous and divine and very, very reasonable. I believe in one thing and one thing only. And that is the divine law of the Rat." Dogma then took out a harmonica, sounded out three notes, and began a slightly robotic song and dance:

The Rat-a-Tat-Tat-Tat
The Rat of Rockets and Pocket Calculators and
*   Freeze-Dried Ice Cream . . .*
The Rat without Good Luck Charms or Fortune Cookies
or Ouija Boards or Magic Crystals
But still, other kinds of crystals, like Gypsum and Beryl,

and snowflakes,
even though they melt.
I follow.
The Rat.
Everywhere.
Unlike you.

Dogma directed *unlike you* right at Downer.
Which made tears appear in Downer's eyes.

Negative Numbers

When someone is mean or hostile or weird to you, it's annoying; when someone is mean or hostile or weird to someone you care about, you might feel like one of those creatures who changes colors and grows muscles and starts yelling and pounding their chest.

This was how Fred felt when she saw Downer in tears.

She also realized on some level, though she might not have admitted it, that her saying "birthday" again and again was not unrelated to their current plight.

Fred stepped up to Dogma and said that she knew for a fact that Downer was the greatest follower of the Rat that ever was, and that he, Dogma, was looking at the White Elephant who risked everything to get the Rat out of the Bag, the White Elephant who—

Dogma said, "I am taking note that you're now at risk of violating Ideally Calm Rat Rule 16, Against Unnecessarily Impassioned Speeches; Ruddy Rat Rule 21, Never Let Your Feelings Overrule the Rule of the Rat; and Subclause 17 of Rat Rule 5, No Making Excuses for Someone Who Is Making Excuses for Someone Else."

Dogma went on: "And you, Downer, are very much risking revocation of the Utterly Perfect Rat Rule 61 regarding an elephant in the room. You don't respect Rat Law as I do, and you don't know Rat Law as I do."

Downer wiped his eyes and glumly interposed: "That is not accurate, Dogma. I know Rat Law backward, I know it forward. I know it in binary code and in Pig Latin. I would know it if it was rolled in mud, covered in leaves and wearing a muumuu—"

"You can't support seventy-eight of seventy-nine Rat rules, Downer; you have to take the whole book. You can't eat seven of eight slices of a pizza," Dogma added flatly. "You have to eat the whole pie."

"I eat plenty of pizza—" Downer said, raising his voice.

"It's either all the pizza or none of the pizza," Dogma growled back at him.

"I've often eaten just a few slices of a pizza," Gogo offered diplomatically. But no one cared.

Dogma took out a notebook and wrote out a ticket in his curiously tidy handwriting. Turning to Fred, he barked: "Rat law is here to protect you. Enforcement is for your benefit. As the Rat says: People who have too many birthdays die. That is inarguable. You're welcome." He handed Fred her golden ticket:

It is kindly demanded that you present yourself to the kangaroo or other available creature court at _____ o'clock on the _____ day of _____ for judgment and sentencing regarding:

SUPER SERIOUS AND REPEATED VIOLATION of THE ESSENTIAL AND VERY GOOD AND NO ONE CAN DISAGREE WITH RAT RULE 79.

Time and Date of Issuance: 11:21 p.m. on Same Old Day as Ever

"Excuse me, but it's blank here?" said Fred. "And here and also here."

"It's not blank," said Dogma.

"Um, it is blank."

"No," said Dogma. "It isn't."

"You're very sure of yourself, aren't you?" observed Fred, annoyed.

"I am."

"You have to at least admit that *I* don't see anything."

"I don't have to admit anything," Dogma said. "What I tell you is that marking time *in the usual ways* is illegal. That's why I don't do it. Still, it's wrong to be late. Even in *the usual ways.*" Dogma then yawned—which seemed odd—and began his exit, a mirror image of his entrance, growing larger as he approached the horizon and then, in the moment when he seemed to be everything, vanishing.

Zeno's Chapter

Dear reader, perhaps you are feeling, as Fred was feeling, annoyed by how ridiculous it was to have a rule against birthdays. But let's avoid being too quick to judge. Have you ever considered how it's impossible to get from one birthday to the next? Think about this. Before you can go all the way from being 12 to being 13, you have to get to halfway between them: $12\frac{1}{2}$. And before you can go all the way from being $12\frac{1}{2}$ to 13, you have to get to halfway between: $12\frac{3}{4}$. And before you can go all the way from being $12\frac{3}{4}$ to 13, you have to get to halfway between: $12\frac{7}{8}$. And then to halfway again—$12\frac{15}{16}$—and to halfway again—$12\frac{31}{32}$—and again and again and again . . . and as you can see, it actually *is* impossible to reach 13, since you keep having to go halfway between first. Right?

A Round Tuit Chapter

Fred's ticketed violation of The Essential and Very Good and No One Can Disagree with Rat Rule 79 was punishable with a bazillion-dollar fine or a century of imprisonment or both. Gogo knew this, and Downer knew this, because they knew and lived under Rat Law. Fred, not being a local, didn't know. (Exactly how you could be put in prison for one hundred and three years when it was illegal to mark the passage of years was a problem to which the Rat was apparently indifferent.) Gogo and Downer, who had little in common, did share a desire to protect Fred from this information. For now.

Fred was studying the ticket. "How can I comply with something I don't even understand?"

Gogo, nibbling on a pickle, said, "I say we deal with this when we get . . . a Round Tuit."

Fred thought longingly again of peanut butter.

Downer was saying, "I've got a pretty long list of things I'm going to do when I get a Round Tuit. I'm going to clean my house when I get a Round Tuit. And learn how to ride a bicycle when I get a Round Tuit. And stop eating only the red gummy bears. Not that anyone should listen to me, since I'm unlovable and no fun to have around. But I agree: let's add dealing with this ticket to that list."

Gogo said, "What do you think, Fred?"

"About what?"

"About the Round Tuit idea?"

"Fine by me," Fred said, confused. Though somewhere in the jumble of her memory, she remembered a wooden coin, one her mother claimed came from the World's Fair. It was round, and had "TUIT" painted on it in red. "We'll worry about the ticket when we get around to it."

I can't speak to the plan of waiting until one gets a Round Tuit, but I do know that it is usually a very, very bad idea to put off thinking about or doing something until you get around to it. Not always, but often enough. That said, I wasn't there with them, and there was nothing I could do to save them from their plans. Fred folded the ticket in half and then in half again and put it in her pajama pocket.

"Hey, look!" she shouted. She started running. "That way!" She was sure she had seen her mom.

At Nothing O'Clock

O
r at least she had seen someone in a skirt that looked like a red-and-white tablecloth, running. Fred's friends followed. They passed through a gap in the mountains, which opened up into a landscape of red stones and dust.

Fred looked left.

She looked right.

She couldn't spot the red-and-white check cloth anywhere. She had heard how travelers lost in the desert often saw water when none was there. Was it only hope, there to frustrate her again? It began to drizzle. Then it began to rain. Then it began to rain even harder.

The trio ran for shelter toward the one building in sight. As they approached, it became clear it wasn't just any old building, but a clocktower. A clocktower with a broken clock. The clocktower was painted pale green, the color of the city swimming pool in some distant city of Fred's childhood. The building looked neglected, with the paint chipping off and tired vines climbing the sides. The clockface had no hands. The beak of a yellow wooden bird peeked out of an open wooden window shutter, as if time had frozen in the middle of the cuckoo-clock show. Next to the clocktower's front door was an overflowing mailbox. Who didn't want to read their mail?

On the clocktower's door hung a sign:

VISITORS NOT WELCOME

On the ground was a doormat labeled

UNWELCOMING MAT

The wind picked up, the rain fell harder. Fred's fluffy bunny slippers were heavy and wet, and she began to shiver. She knocked at the door. There were no trees, no boulders large enough to hide behind.

"Wrong consonant!" a voice shouted out from inside the clocktower house.

Not her mother's voice. Definitely not.

"Wrong continent?"

"I think he said Incompetent," Downer mumbled. "I get called that sometimes. It's okay."

"Con-so-nant!" the voice from within shouted again. "Wrong consonant, you fools!"

"I think he's saying consonant," Gogo offered. "How weird."

"Maybe he means it," Fred offered, "like croissants are *consonant* with chocolate. Or peanut butter is *consonant* with pickles? People don't know how good peanut butter is with pickles. Or that 'consonant' can be used that—"

"What I'm saying is, Go away!" the voice shouted.

"It's raining really hard out here," Fred pleaded with the door.

"Are you likely to die out there?" the voice inquired.

"Probably not," Fred admitted.

"Or be seriously injured? Or suffer grave emotional damage from which it will take years to recover? Or develop a life-long fear of the damp? Such that you can't eat mushrooms, or oatmeal?"

"We'll just be very uncomfortable and unhappy," Fred said. "That's probably the worst of it."

The door opened. "At least you're honest," the creature behind the door said. "Honesty opens the door," he sighed. "That's the little celebrated Rat Rule 8."

Picky Mouse's Tale

The keeper of the non-functioning clocktower was a mouse named Picky Mouse. Picky was a moderate-sized mouse. He wore green pants and white gloves. He brought out cushions for his guests, whom he seated in polished wooden chairs arranged around a kitchen table covered in a sweet yellow-and-white gingham tablecloth. Not the same tablecloth Fred and her mom shared at home, but similar. Picky Mouse took Fred's fluffy bunny slippers from her feet, sponged off the reddish mud, and set them to dry by the fireplace in a back room. Then he put on a little apron and prepared and served hot chocolate with miniature colored marshmallows.

"For someone with an Unwelcoming Mat at his door, you're pretty nice," said Fred. She said this even though, personally, she didn't like marshmallows.

Downer and Gogo murmured agreement. And they did like marshmallows.

The kind words must have touched Picky Mouse's heart, for after a few spoonfuls of cocoa, and learning that these friends were headed to the Rat, Picky Mouse began to open up:

"I worked for the Rat for many years. I might still work for the Rat. We always got along well. My job used to be keeping this clocktower working. You may have noticed outside that it's not working anymore. The Rat was very good with things like clocks, as you may know. But when The Essential and Very Good and No One Can Disagree with Rat Rule 79 was passed I didn't know what to do. All the Rat told me was that time needed to stop. *No more time*, she said in a huff. *It's over!* I was afraid to ask for clarification; she was very difficult at the time of that Rule, as you may recall; many of us thought it was almost as if she weren't herself. But what could we do? We had sworn our devotion, and she had done so much for us."

"That's true," Downer said.

"Anyhow, that was when it became my job to keep the clocktower *not* working. At least I thought that was my job. I was guessing. One of my friends had the courage to ask, very politely, *Excuse me, I'm not quite sure I follow?* At which the Rat shouted, '**I want it abolished. Now!**'

"Of course, we were too afraid to mention that abolishing time could be a bit tricky, or that to abolish it 'now' was to say 'at this time,' which doesn't make much sense if you've just erased the difference between the present, the past, and the future. And it did turn out to be tricky. Time is valuable, precious—so precious that people steal it. And now suddenly time was worthless. Worse—it was illegal to have time on your hands or to keep time in any way. So there was a total collapse of the time market. Not only did no one want to steal time anymore, no one wanted to buy it either. Everyone with time on their hands wanted to sell it but couldn't. *Your time is your own*, I would tell people who came to me asking for advice. But of course they were worried they would get in trouble for having all that time to spend. So the only thing we could do was waste our time. That was the worst. Have you ever tried to waste your time—waste all of it? It's very, very difficult. Something ends up being worthwhile, it turns out the time hasn't been wasted at all, and then you have to start all over again. But since she was the Rat Queen, we all tried our best. For my part, I decided that I would no longer give anyone the time of day."

Our friends had been listening to Picky Mouse's story closely and sympathetically.

Picky Mouse added, "I'm sorry I was rude at the door. As you can see, you caught me at a bad time." He sipped his cocoa.

"Your story gets me so angry—" Gogo said, raising her fists.

"And makes me so sad—" Downer said, wiping his eye.

"Do you still like your work?" Fred asked.

"I wouldn't say I'm having the time of my life," Picky Mouse said. "But, yes, I do still like being the timekeeper. But I'm not actually keeping time, of course, because that would be illegal. I've completely lost track of time. And that's one reason I don't like to let folks in here, because they'll see"—he gestured around the old-fashioned interior—"that I've run out of time like everyone else. Keeping people out, though, has left me pretty lonely. It's just me, myself, and I in here. Oh, and the Time Flies." At the window, gentle flies with translucent pink wings were busying themselves in apparently aimless flights and landings.

It was still raining.

Having finished her hot cocoa, Fred shivered.

"You're a child, aren't you?" asked Picky Mouse.

"Sort of," Fred said. "Like, in part."

"How nice to see you in these parts. Many children fled Rat Rule 79, of course. Understandable. Your slippers might be dry now," Picky Mouse said.

In the back, Fred found her bunny slippers still slightly damp. She decided to sit and wait a few minutes more for them to dry. *What an absurd Rat these creatures follow*, thought Fred, as she mused about the apparent dubious legality of waiting "a few minutes more." And what was that about the children fleeing? Fred warmed her hands by the fire and enjoyed the quiet company of the Time Flies. Something in the way they flitted, and even in the way they landed, seemed joyful. One landed on a dusty pile of papers, rubbed its wings together craftily, then took off again.

The dusty pile of papers turned out to be a dusty pile of invitations.

Or, rather, Un-Invitations. Fred read, **You Are Cordially Un-Invited to . . .**

The un-invitation date was that of Fred's own birthday.

Were you even allowed to mark down a date like that?

The border of the un-invitations was done in looping red lines.

Fred put on her still damp slippers. She picked up one of the Un-invitations. Then she took the rest of them, too. They were too large to fit in her pajama pockets, so she tucked them awkwardly into the waistband of her pajama pants. It's true that another word for what Fred did was steal.

Two wrongs may not make a right, she said to herself, *but three rights do make a left.* It was something her mom used to say. *And three lefts make a right. And no one likes to be left behind.*

Chapter Chance

F red did eventually solve the dot problem her mom had given her. By accident.

She had sat down at lunch alone. (She would want to be clear: she didn't mind eating lunch alone, especially not when she had a peanut butter and pickle sandwich on raisin bread, which was much nicer to eat without having anyone questioning your taste.) When she had finished her sandwich, she still had another fifteen minutes. She took out a pen and used her lunch bag to once again draw the nine-dot puzzle her mother had given her like a coded message. She made several attempts:

  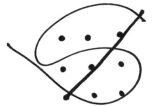

While she was beginning another try, a boy named Milo Mungle bumped her arm as he walked behind her. She liked Milo Mungle because he had a nice smile and also because his name made it seem like he was from a poem where he was king of the jungle. The Mungle arm-bumping caused Fred's pen to move, which left her with:

Whereupon, she found herself coming up with this:

Which made her feel like *she* was king of the jungle.

The Present Chapter

Returning to the main room, Fred discreetly slipped the Un-invitations into Gogo's backpack. They might prove useful—in time.

"Come with us to free the Rat," Downer was saying to Picky Mouse, as Fred returned to her seat at the table. "If the Rat hears your tale, she'll make things better, I know she will."

"The Rat Queen doesn't listen to reason," Picky Mouse said, shaking his head.

"She's the Rat *of* Reason," Downer argued. "You're wrong."

"I wish I was wrong," said Picky Mouse. "You don't know the Rat the way I do. She's not who she thinks she is!"

"She'll listen to you," Downer went on. "You're her Timekeeper, for goodness sake, of course she'll listen to you. She'll see what's wrong with The Essential and Very Good and No One Can Disagree with Rat Rule 79, and she'll amend it, I'm sure of it. Come with us, please."

"I'm better off here with the Time Flies," Picky Mouse said. "More fun. But there is one thing of which I have plenty to give since the Rat Queen made the future illegal." He reached under the table. "Here," Picky Mouse said, "is the Present." The Present was wrapped in silver paper with large blue polka dots. "No need to open it now. Keep it for when you need it. A little something to make up for the time you lost here with me."

Chapter Twelve Thousand Four Hundred and Seven, the Officially Most Boring Number in the World

By evening the rain had cleared. "I've figured out where we are on this map," Gogo said. "If we can get to The Land You Can Only Get to Through Sleep, we should be in great shape."

Gogo set out a plastic tarp on the damp green lawn in front of the non-working clocktower. Then our friends lay down on it and worked and worked on getting to sleep for what seemed to them like hours, perhaps even days. Since there were no functioning watches or clocks—the clocktower face told an eternal everytime—they didn't really know how long exactly. They didn't know, but I know. What felt like a near-eternity to them was thirty-six minutes. To be fair, Trying to Go to Sleep is way more difficult than Falling Asleep. If Going to Sleep is like a falling feather making its way to you, then Trying to Go to Sleep is like a gust of wind, a bunch of gusts in a row, blowing that feather off course again and again. Telling someone to try to go to sleep is pretty much the equivalent of turning on all the lights and inviting in a marching band with an overeager cymbals player who doesn't know how to keep tempo. Or so thought Fred, as she Tried to Go to Sleep. It was impossible. More evidence, she thought sourly, of how dumb her mother's go-to solution of A Good Night's Sleep was. Or her idea of Knowing You're Loved—but Fred's unsleepy red thoughts were interrupted by Gogo, tapping her, saying: "*You* must have some really boring stories."

"What? Why do you think *my* stories are boring?"

"We *want* boring stories," Downer explained, "so that we can fall asleep. I can also tell boring stories, but I'm so boring that it becomes interesting. Interesting in how boring I can be."

Gogo said, "Our asking you to tell a boring story is a compliment, Fred. We're saying you're powerful."

"Flattering," Fred said sulkily. "But I can't think of a boring story."

"Boring things?" Downer said.

Fred considered. "Watching cabbage grow can be pretty boring. I used to have a cabbage plant in the yard—we hadn't even planted it; it was just there. Several times a day I would go out to the yard to see if I could catch the cabbages in their moment of growing—"

"I love cruciferous vegetables," lamented Gogo. "I find cabbage to be a really exciting topic, please stop."

"You know what I think is boring?" Downer said glumly. "All the words that sound like dull. They make my mouth sleepy. Lull. Mull. Cull."

"Wull," Gogo said.

"Wull?"

"Kruller," Fred said.

"Kruller?"

"It's a kind of donut—"

"Oh, I love donuts—" Gogo said.

"And I love almost-rhymes," Downer said. "Like . . .
excitable."

"Excitable rhymes with dull?"

"Kind of," Downer said.

"How about water bowl?" Gogo said.

"I've got it!" Fred nearly shouted. "Video games are boring."

Downer gave Fred a hard stare. "That is totally untrue."

"What about tooth-brushing?" Gogo offered.

"Nah."

"Candy?"

"How is candy boring?"

They were having no luck, getting bored. Eventually, the
moon rose, moody and familiar. Fred pointed and said: "It's
a croissant moon."

"Crescent moon," Downer corrected.

Correcting someone is a pretty dull thing to do.

"Croissant moon," Fred further corrected. "I know other
people call it crescent. But in my home we call it croissant."

"Whatever," Gogo said, stretching her arms and yawning.

"I miss my mom," Fred said.

"That's a good one," Downer said with an admiring yawn.
"That's super boring."

Gogo agreed, with an additional yawn of her own. She lay
down on her back. "Missing your mom. Thank you. What

a good idea. Tell us more about how you feel. That will put me right to sleep."

Fred could have been offended, but she wasn't. She lay down and said quietly, "Well, I feel kind of bad that I yelled at her. Even though I still think she was wrong, and annoying. I wonder why she came here. If she needed a break from me. I wonder if she's okay."

Downer's eyelids fluttered. Gogo's head tipped against a nearby tree. The only one still awake was Fred, beneath the flaky, croissant moon. Then, at some point, she wasn't awake anymore. Did she dream a useful or interesting or boring dream? A scary one? A flying one? A monstrous one? That's none of our business. That she gets to keep to herself.

Chapter $\sqrt{-1}$

To her not quite surprise, Fred awoke near a large stone building, one that hadn't been there when she'd fallen asleep. Around her was a chilly valley scented by pine trees. Was this the Land You Could Only Get to Through Sleep? Was today her birthday? Or was it still the same day it was before? The sky held perfectly puffy white clouds. Fred recognized the landscape but couldn't place it. Had she and her mom visited here? Purchased a souvenir purple-handled miniature fork and spoon at an unseen gas station nearby? Whereas the clocktower had been swimming-pool green, this stone building was grocery-bag brown. Some might have termed the great dark stone building a castle; others not so much. Was this the Bag? Fred definitely wouldn't have named it that, even if it was the color of a (brown paper) bag.

Fred shook Downer. Downer apologized for snoring, and Fred told him he wasn't snoring, and then he said so why did you wake me up, and she said she wanted his company, and he said that was very weird and that he didn't believe her and that he was going to try to sleep some more.

Fred then went to shake Gogo; Gogo begged for five more minutes.

Fred's mom also often begged for a few more minutes of sleep. It struck Fred again the way adults were at once so sleepy, but also so often insisting that it was the young people—perfectly alert and awake—who needed to go to bed on time. On time! What time? It was a real mystery that masqueraded as not a mystery.

"I'm sorry about that snoring," Downer said, now up and about.

"You weren't snoring."

"I'm sure I was bothering you one way or another," he sighed.

Downer and Fred made their way over to the dark stone building, as Gogo slept in. On an oversized wooden door, there hung a sign:

RAT VISITING HOURS: 3:30 PM TO 3:30 PM[1]

"Does 3:30 p.m. to 3:30 p.m. mean always? Or never?" Fred asked.

"Oh it doesn't even matter," Downer sighed over Fred's shoulder. "I knew this was hopeless. It'll never be 3:30 p.m."

"It feels that way sometimes, I know," Fred said.

"I'm not talking about feelings," Downer said. "I'm talking about *Ferlings*. It will never be 3:30 p.m. because of the Ferlings."

"Because timekeeping is illegal?" Fred asked.

Downer shook his large head. "Not that. Follow the footnotes." With his trunk, he indicated a lower line of the sign:

¹ RAT EXEMPT FROM RAT RULE 79²

"Hey, *she's* exempt—but I'm in trouble just for saying, you know, the word I said?"

Downer pointed to the next footnote:

² BECAUSE RAT LIVES UNDER FEARSOME FERLING RULE, NOT UNDER RIGHTEOUS RAT RULE³

"That's not fair," Fred said.

Downer pointed to the even smaller writing, further down:

³ THEREFORE FEARSOME FERLING STANDARD TIME APPLIES TO RAT, NOT RAT STANDARD NON-TIME.

"It's hard for you because you're not used to failure the way I am. I'm accustomed to failure," Downer said. "I take pride in being accustomed to failure. But still: this feels bad. To be so close to the Rat and yet hit this impossible obstacle. I guess I should have expected this." At that, Downer began the saddest little soft-shoe dance ever:

> *Oh Ratty Rat Rat*
> *I won't blackmail you*
> *But I will fail you*
> *I won't sail you*
> *Or manage to bail you . . .*

Gogo had awoken and hurried over, her backpack slung over one shoulder. "Well this scene looks sadder than a jellyfish in the Sahara. What's wrong?"

"Gogo, do you know what time it is now in Fearsome Ferling Standard Time?" Fred asked.

"Sure," Gogo said. "Fearsome Ferling Standard Time is whatever time you feel like it is."

"Really?"

"The Ferlings are all about whatever you feel like."

"Great!" said Fred. She turned to Downer: "As soon as we're all ready, I'll say I feel like it's 3:30 p.m."

"You can't fake your feelings, Fred," Downer said.

"Oh, sure I can—"

"I don't mean *you* can't fake your feelings," Downer said with a tear. "I mean it doesn't work that way. Your feelings are whatever they are, even if you pretend they're something else. That's one of the reasons feelings are so annoying, and Ferlings take advantage of—"

"Let me see this sign," Gogo interrupted impatiently. "You two are hopeless. I'm sure we can solve—"

But as soon as Gogo got a gander at the sign, she started to sneeze again. She pulled out a kerchief from her very useful orange backpack. (It was a mysteriously familiar kerchief, with a red-and-white check pattern.) Fred was worried that Gogo would notice the stolen Un-Invitations, but the mongoose didn't let on about anything. Perhaps because she was so busy sneezing.

"Bless you," Downer said to the sneezing Gogo triumphantly—by which I mean, with the happiness of the pessimist who can finally declare that his pessimism was justified, and he wasn't just being a downer. "See, Fred, even Gogo can see that it's hopeless. Rest assured, we'll never reach the Rat now. I don't know why we tried. Fearsome Ferling Time is famously impossible to navigate. Even if we manage to feel like it's 3:30 p.m.—and it's very difficult to feel like it's exactly 3:30 p.m.—there is no way of ensuring that the Rat will feel like it's 3:30 p.m. along with us. You can't just tell other people how to feel. I mean, you can try, but it never works. And. . . ."

Downer continued to detail his pessimism. Gogo continued to sneeze her anxiety. But Fred felt she was beginning to understand the Land of Impossibility. It wasn't so impossible. It was a world where words were annoyingly powerful. A world where even a bright little word like *birthday* was seen as a major problem. She thought of the Know-It-Owl, who meant exactly what she said. And who confused others by assuming that they did, too.

That was when she had an idea. Another possible solution.

"We've forgotten something!" Fred exclaimed. "We've forgotten the Present!"

Taking Gogo's backpack from her, Fred rummaged past the Un-Invitations, past several handkerchiefs, past a jar of pickles—that backpack could hold so much!—until finally she found the polka-dotted box tied with silver ribbon that Picky Mouse had given them.

Fred set the Present on the ground before them.

"Here," she said, pointing to the gift. "I don't mean to sound like a Know-It-Owl, but what I'm thinking is that there's no time like the Present."

Chapter =

Inside the box was an old wristwatch with a cracked face. It was not ticking. Nor was it tocking. It was, in that sense, a well-behaved wristwatch from the Realm of the Rat.

The watch had a cute mouse at the center of its face—a mouse that looked a lot like Picky Mouse. Two mouse arms, one longer and one shorter, pointed to the numbers of the hours. Picky looked so happy on the watch face, so proud to be keeping time.

"Yup, it's broken," Downer said.

They stood around the non-working watch, looking at it.

"How are you feeling now, Miss Hopeful?" Downer said.

"Don't tick me off, elephant," Gogo said, and then sneezed again.

"I'm glad it doesn't work," Fred said with a small frown. "Otherwise we would have been carrying contraband all this time. Right? I'm in enough trouble already. This is good news," she said, without conviction.

Gogo gave a further little achoo. "You know what would be more annoying than wasps at a watering hole? If someone were to say right now *When life gives you lemons, make lemonade.*"

More time passed—or whatever passes for time in a timeless land. The smile on the watch-mouse's face stayed true.

115

"What you said is really smart, Gogo," Fred said.

"It is?" said Gogo.

"About the lemons. This gift is a lemon, right?"

Downer said, "If you mean lemon as in citrus fruit once relied upon to keep sailors healthy at sea, then no. If you mean lemon as in useless and no-good? Then yes."

Fred continued, "We know Picky Mouse wouldn't give us a useless and no-good gift—"

"I'm not sure we do know that," interrupted Gogo.

"My preferred term for a useless, no-good gift is a White Elephant," added Downer.

"This gift *is* useful," Fred insisted. "I know it is. We just need to figure out the right way to use it." She began to chew at her nails and pace back and forth, and back and forth, like she was stalking a solution.

"Ouch!" Gogo said, as Fred stumbled on her toe.

"Sorry," Fred said, and stopped pacing and chewing her nails.

"I know Children Are the Best Thing in the World and everything, but you could be a little more careful—"

"Wait, I've got it!" Fred said. In her excitement she accidentally knocked Gogo over, making her lockets clatter and jangle. "Sorry about that." She picked Gogo up in her arms and climbed onto Downer's back. "Now, Downer, please step on the watch!"

"What? No way." Downer didn't want to be the guy who breaks things, the guy with four left feet. He hated feeling like a bulldozer with big ears, a bull in a china shop.

"I like the watch, too," Gogo said from on high. "I could give it to Mango. Or Django. Or Bingo. Bingo loves broken watches. So does Bob, now that I think about it."

"Please," Fred said. "Trust me. Step on it. Don't you see? If you step on it, with me and Gogo on top of you—we'll all be Right on Time."

"Oh this is really not going to go well," whimpered Downer. "I really don't think I should do this." But he did.

Chapter 1729

There was once a great mathematician from India named Ramanujan who was sick in the hospital. This is a true story, by the way. Ramanujan's friend, also a mathematician, a man named Hardy, went to visit him. The taxicab that Hardy took to the hospital bore the number 1729. When Hardy arrived, he told Ramanujan the taxi number, which seemed to Hardy like a particularly uninteresting number. He hoped that wasn't a bad sign for his unwell friend.

Ramanujan answered straight away that 1729 *was* a very interesting number. He said it was the smallest number that was expressible as the sum of two cubes, in two different ways. (That is, $1^3+12^3=1729$, and also $9^3+10^3=1729$.)

Look, I'm not a human calculator either. But anybody can see that there was something magical in how quickly Ramanujan knew that about 1729. With that magically speedy insight, he had turned what seemed like a sign of bad luck—a boring number—into a sign of good luck—an interesting number.

One funny and perhaps sad detail here is that Hardy was not only a good friend but also someone who had a remarkably beautiful face. Everyone who knew him said so. Hardy, though, found his face so ugly that he avoided all mirrors. So Hardy was himself a kind of 1729. Ramanujan could see his special qualities; Hardy himself could not.

Why am I telling you this? Because I have a hard time talking about Downer. He is dear to my heart, even if he doesn't know it or feel it. Instead, he is sure nobody likes him. Let me tell you a little a secret of Downer's. The last time he had set out in search of the Rat—with the intention, as you know, of letting the Rat out of the Bag—he . . . well, he only got as far as the bus stop down the block. From there, Downer was escorted to the dungeon by a band of mice wearing pink jerseys. Predictable, in its way. Not only because Downer was convinced that things would never go well for him (and when you're convinced things won't go well, that often ensures that they won't), but also because he had hardly made a secret of his plans to Free the Rat. He told anyone who would listen about his plans. He sang and did a soft-shoe dance with an umbrella about them. Perhaps Downer, in some way, had known the mission would go badly, that he would not be able to Free the Rat. Perhaps that was why he had chosen the mission—because he was most comfortable when things went wrong.

Real Numbers

"**I** hope you won't let the cat out of the bag about this," a steady voice said.

The words reached our friends across the complete dark. Fred's plan had worked; they had arrived right on time. But arrived where? They could see neither hand nor foot nor paw. There was no breeze or scent of pine. The darkness was so disorienting that Fred wondered if the voice was coming from inside her head.

"Why would someone put a cat *in* a bag?" Fred asked aloud to the darkness.

They heard a dry laugh. "I don't have to mean what I say. Not here. There's no real cat, and no real bag. Just little old me. And a very boring secret that I hope you won't tell." The voice coughed.

"We're not here to give away anyone's secrets, we promise," Fred said, with a quiver in her voice. "We're here to see the Rat."

No response.

"The Ratty-Rat-Rat of Rationality and Reason and Raisins and Rockets," Fred clarified.

"Interesting," said the voice.

"The Rat who helped my friend Downer, the elephant in the room. The Rat who will pay this mongoose mother of seventeen for her work freeing us from the dungeon. The Rat who will help me find my mom."

"You sound very convinced," said the voice. "That's sweet. That you have such hopes for the Rat Queen."

There was a click, a reading lamp was lit, and a furriness in a rocking chair was illuminated. The furriness was gnawing on an old crushed aluminum can. The furriness was, Fred noticed, surrounded by piles of . . . garbage. Old orange peels, crumpled-up paper bags, coffee grounds. And yet Fred could also distinctly make out the scent of chocolate croissants. And peanut butter. And pickles. What she wouldn't give for a peanut butter and pickle sandwich right about now.

"Nice slippers," the furry creature said. "Does that mean you are a Child? Children are the Best Thing in the World."

"Um, thanks," said Fred, looking down at her feet. Again she had forgotten she was in her pajamas. "They're from when—" Fred stopped speaking as she noticed that the creature was wearing a red-and-white check robe, one that looked like her tablecloth, and like the skirt she had seen her mother in. "I like your robe. . . . Excuse me, but: Are *you* the Rat Queen?"

The creature took another bite of aluminum can.

Fred looked at Gogo, who looked at Downer, who looked back at Fred.

The garbage-eating creature set down her snack. "I suppose I owe all of you an apology," she said.

The travelers didn't say anything. But Fred, again, started to nervously bite at her nails. Then she noticed she was biting at her nails, and stopped biting them.

The Rat—as Fred suspected, this garbage-gnawing creature *was* the Rat—then said, "Did you hear me? I said I owe
all of you an apology. Now one of you say: *If you say so.*"

Neither Fred, nor Downer, nor Gogo knew what to say.
Even though they had just been told what to say.

The Rat Queen said again, louder: "You say: *If you say so.*
And then I say: *Yes, I say so.*"

Our friends remained silent.

"Come on," the Rat said. "Please. I used to do this with
Hart all the time. Hart loved our back-and-forth. Oh, Hart.
Dear, dear Hart. Hart also was The Best Thing in the World.
Hart also was once a child. Maybe Go ahead: say *If you say so.*"

"Heart?" Fred asked. "Who's Heart?"

Gogo shrugged; she looked downcast.

Downer, however, did speak up. For once, he didn't look
downcast; he looked mad. "Pardon me, Ratty-Rat of Rhubarb
Jam and Rudders. But I'm not going to say, *If you say so.*"

"There: you said it," the Rat said. "Thank you. As a reward,
I will tell you my story."

Once Upon a Time

As you may have noticed, dear reader, there were no Ferlings guarding the Rat in that rocking chair. There were no locks on the door, no snarling dogs at a gate. Just a melancholy creature, in a red-and-white check robe, in a very, very untidy room. A nonsensical sign about visiting times kept visitors out—but what kept the Rat in? How were our friends supposed to feel, seeing that so much of what they had heard about the Ratty Rat Rat was, shall we say, less than true? Who had spread the rumors of her captivity? Why did she eat metal? Couldn't she sweep the floor now and again?

"Much of what gets said about me, and sung about me, was once true," the shabby Rat Queen began. "It really was. I *did* correct the aim of rockets. I *did* keep bridges from collapsing. I *did* come up with the best way to stack oranges in crates. The rise and fall of the sea, the dance of the honeybee, I before E except after C—I understood all of that. I helped other people understand it, too. Treat Others the Way You would Want to Be Treated Yourself? That was my brainwave. I am proud to say that I was the most rational of Rats, and I used that rationality in the most rational of ways. I don't mean to boast, but I was rightly termed a Righteous Queen. My Rule Book for Living wasn't perfect—I get it. But it was pretty good. I gave what I had and much of what I gave was good. Don't you think, Downer?"

124

Our mournful pachyderm averted his eyes. (A pachyderm is a thick-skinned animal, for example a hippopotamus or rhinoceros or . . . elephant. You, dear reader, are almost certainly not a pachyderm.)

"The problems began when I lost Hart . . . I'm a puddle now. Or a muddle. Or a fuddle, because I feel befuddled? When I try to think clearly, I feel like I'm being punched in the head by a school of stale octopuses."

"Wouldn't that be stale octo*pi*?" Downer asked, very politely.

"I don't think octopi go stale, Rat Queen," offered Gogo, who was quietly chewing a pickle. "If I may say so. Respectfully."

"They don't?" the Rat said. "Well, there you go. That's the kind of mistake I make these days. I'm in a buddle."

Fred took one of Gogo's pickles and tried to stay hopeful, even as she longed for peanut butter and bread to make a perfectly comforting sandwich. She asked the Rat a less Ratty question. An important question. "Rat Queen, why did you lose heart?"

Taking a pickle as well, the Rat wiped a tear from her face. "My *Hart*, not my heart." The Rat pulled a chalkboard out from the garbage around her and wrote *Hart*, then drew a heart beneath the name. "I lost my dear deer."

You see, dear reader, hart is another name for a deer. It used to be a common name. Now almost no one uses it. Why would they? It's old-fashioned and confusing. A hart is different from a heart, obviously, even though of course a hart has a heart. You get the point.

"When I first met Hart, he was just a tiny little fawn," the Rat said. "He showed up at my doorstep. His legs were still wobbly. I offered him some apple. Then some pecans. The next day some sweet potato. He was shy at first, but he was curious, too. And hungry, I suppose. That little fawn started to come by every day. Every day and then, finally, most of the day every day.

"I never meant to be a mother. It wasn't my plan. I was busy being the most Rational Rat of Rattiness. I didn't need to love another creature. I was happy alone. But then there Hart was, and he was so young and so little, and needed me in a way no one else ever had. Even when I would use the restroom—I wasn't an ordinary Rat, I liked a little quiet time in the bathroom—Hart would stand outside the door mewing and bleating and banging his delicate fawn head against the door until I came out. He didn't want to be separated from me even for a minute! Same thing when I sat down in a chair to read a book. Or spoke to any creature other than Hart. He wanted to play counting games with me. He wanted to cuddle. He wanted to stack sticks. He wanted to lay around and say nonsense words to each other and giggle. It was exhausting of course—even annoying!—but I was so, so happy."

Downer offered the Rat a tissue.

She blew her nose fiercely and continued: "And then one day." She sniffled. "Well." She snuffled. "One day. One day Hart. . . ." Another tear appeared. "Sorry, this is difficult for me to remember. . . ." The Rat wiped her eyes again; she took a nibble of old orange peel; she swallowed dramatically. "One day I went to the bathroom, and Hart didn't follow me in! He stayed outside, building a tepee out of some popsicle sticks I had lying around." The Rat sniffled more. "He was perfectly content *on his own* even though I was in the bathroom for many, many seconds—maybe even a minute!"

Fred was thinking, but not saying: Well, of course that would happen. Hart was *growing up.*

The Rat eyed Fred. "I know what you're thinking. You're thinking, 'Well, of course that would happen. Hart was growing up.'"

Fred said, "Um—"

The Rat suddenly stood up on her hind legs and triumphantly pointed a claw upward. "Growing up is wrong! It never stops!"

Gogo wiped a tear from her eye, too. She shook her head. She kissed the lockets with her photos of her children one by one.

The Rat wiped her eyes with an old sock and continued: "When he was little, Hart would wake up and say to me, 'What did *we* dream last night?' Because he thought of us as One. I would tell him that I couldn't know what he dreamed, that his dreams were his own; he would laugh at me and tell me that wasn't true. That lasted for a while. He told me that we dreamed of jellyfish once. I would never dream of jellyfish! Jellyfish with many eyes, he said. But then one morning he woke up and told me that *he* had a dream. Not 'we.' 'What kind of dream?' I asked. 'A funny dream,' he said. And then he said he couldn't tell me more because, because"—here Rat started wailing—"it was a secret."

Three loud sneezes signaled Gogo's mood.

"Bless you." The Rat Queen went on: "Soon his antlers were coming in. He learned to run faster. He made friends with a chipmunk who lived down the way. A nice chipmunk. *Too* nice. They stayed out for hours, the two of them, building forts. Nibbling on wild berries and onion grasses. Trading jokes about chickens crossing roads. Sometimes Hart wouldn't even chat with me when he came home. . . ."

That last word looks normal, but Rat *bawled* it, so that it came out as *hooooooooooome.*

Snuffling and sobs filled the room.

A Normal Chapter

O nly Fred was dry-eyed. And confused. To her mind, the Rat was telling a pretty ordinary story. About a little deer getting bigger. What kind of a tragedy was that? Would there be a fatal bee sting? Or a hunter? She was still waiting for the part of the story where the Hart ran into an electric fence, or broke a leg, or at the very least failed his math exam. *Something* bad must have happened.

The Rat Queen said, "When I think back, I regret how little patience I had with Hart's questions. *Why is water so flat? When do numbers end? What are mean people for? Why can't I eat only chocolate ice cream?* How I would love to hear those questions now, even if he asked them again and again and again and again."

Gogo blew her nose with a honking sound, Downer with a hinking sound, and the Rat with a sort of *hazow, hazow.* Fred started to space out, in her Fred way. She thought about a doll she used to have, with green eyes, whom she had called Green Eyes. She hadn't seen Green Eyes for years; where could she have gone? Was Green Eyes with that round coin that had TUIT written on it in red letters? What about that little fire truck that was also an eraser? Where was the bead necklace of many colors but with one golden bead that was larger than the other beads? What about the fuzzy puffy pumpkin stickers she had saved? Where were the overalls with the small rainbow on them? Where was her foam sword? Her deep interest in penguins? Her detailed knowledge of the moons of Saturn? Where had all that stuff gone? For that matter, where had her mom—

Something was shaking Fred's arm. It was Downer, whispering: "Pay attention!"

The Rat was saying: " . . . so you can see why I decreed that time could no longer pass. You understand, right? You understand the Essential and Very Good and No One Can Disagree with Rat Rule 79 now? I had no choice. I made that decree the day before Hart's . . . well, I'm allowed to say it, since I'm the Ruler . . . before his Birthday. Hart was angry, of course. Every young person loves their Birthday. But sometimes you have to make sacrifices for the greater good. Clearly it would be a tragedy if Hart—if any creature!—were allowed to get older. Children Are the Best Thing in the World, right? And we all know that too many birthdays can kill you. They do. It's a fact! Do you know anyone who doesn't die after too many birthdays? Not to mention that it's easier to remember your age if you don't change it all the time. Hart should have been thanking me. Everyone should be thanking me." She blew her nose. "But no one is thanking me. And Hart stormed out of the house, and I haven't seen him since."

She paused and, this time using an old watermelon rind, wiped tears from her ratty eyes. When she spoke again, her voice was different, softer. "Please don't tell anyone that I'm not being held captive by the Fearsome Ferlings. Please don't tell anyone that I'm just really, really, really, really, really, really sad. I had no choice but to hide away. Even though I did the right thing with The Essential and Very Good and No One Can Disagree with Rat Rule 79. I'm not wrong, right? If I let children grow up, then there would be no children left anymore. It's either No Children or No Birthdays. Either Left or Right. Either Right or Wrong."

A Middle Chapter

I briefly interrupt here not only to remind you that I exist, but also to share a story I once heard about a donkey. The donkey was standing exactly between two identical stacks of delicious (to the donkey) hay. When I say "exactly between," I mean *exactly* between. People have different ideas about what happened next. Some say the donkey ate from the haystack on the left. Others, from the haystack on the right. One or the other. However, many, many people—some with mustaches, some with glasses, some who like to raise tomato plants—say the donkey remained in the middle and eventually starved to death. They argue that presented with two equally appealing options, the donkey couldn't decide which option to choose. He couldn't decide because he never made decisions randomly or irrationally. Thus, death by starvation. Because he was too devoted to being rational. Even the most rattily laid plans have problems like this one lurking inside them.

A Reasonable Chapter

Fred wasn't going to fall for the Rat's way of thinking. "Um, where did you get that red-and-white check robe?" Fred asked the Rat Queen.

"Oh, this old thing," the Rat Queen said. "I can't even remember."

"You can't help me find my mom, can you?"

The Rat Queen continued rocking in her chair, fidgeting with the aluminum can in her claws. "Your mom? That's touching that you're interested in your mom. I wish more children were interested in their moms. Children Are the Best Thing in the World, like I always say, but for most children, mothers are invisible dishrags—"

"Why do people think you're being held captive by Ferlings? I don't see a single Ferling here," she said, not that she knew what a Ferling looked like.

"Well . . . . Okay, I started that rumor," the Rat Queen admitted, rocking in her chair. "I started that rumor so I could be alone here in this Bag of Garbage. I mean, This Castle. Whatever you want to call it."

"So you lied."

The Rat Queen raised her voice and stood up from her rocking chair. "Without my Hart, I'm as useful as a chocolate teapot!" Then more quietly: "I lied about being held captive, sure. But there was a truth in that lie: My woe is a prison. My sadness is a slammer. Melancholy is my master. To be down-cast is to be in a dungeon. And so on. That counts, right?"

To be honest, Fred didn't feel much sympathy. She started pacing in front of the Rat's rocking chair. Pacing and chewing her nails and thinking. If only I had a peanut butter and pickle sandwich, she thought, then I could *really* think . . . Still, she was beginning to understand. . . . *To be downcast is to be in a dungeon* . . . "So who put Downer in a dungeon, then, if it wasn't done by the supposed Ferlings keeping you captive?"

The Rat Queen sighed. "I can't help but admire your logical thinking, child. It was me, okay? I sent Dogma out with a team to do it. You know Dogma? He believes in me wholly. Not partially, but wholly. I knew Downer had the best intentions in wanting to free me. But I couldn't bear to have Downer, or anyone else, discover my secret—that I'm here of my own will." The Rat gestured around the room. "Well, the secret is now plain for you all to see. I know what I did was wrong. But I didn't leave him in the dungeon! In the end, I got him out, didn't I?"

Downer was hiding his face behind his umbrella. He was trying to be an elephant in the room in the old-fashioned way—pretending he wasn't there.

Fred turned back to the Rat: "You didn't get Downer out," she said in a temper. "Gogo got him out."

"I get it now," Gogo said. "*You* sent me that unsigned tip about the Hart being in the dungeon. You sent me the wrong information. To get me to do the right thing. The right thing that you didn't have the courage to do yourself."

"Details!" the Rat muttered. "I hatched the plans! I was the rescuer! Me, me, me, me, me, me!" She sounded like a little kid, but not in a good way. Not in the Children Are the Best Thing in the World way, but in a very-long-line-for-a-roller-coaster-temper-tantrum way.

Fred held the **Wanted: Alive or Alive** poster in front of the Rat Queen's face. "This doesn't count as help! You're mean and selfish and have no idea how others feel. We came all this way for you. We actually had *hope*. It's your *fault* we felt hope. I should have known I would be surprised. And not in a good way." She started kicking the trash that lay scattered around the room. Fred almost added, *And tomorrow's even my birthday!* but she didn't say that, not only because she knew there was a rule against saying *birthday*, but also because she wasn't even sure what day it was. It might already be her birthday. None of it seemed to matter anymore. She had thought she had nothing and nobody before she entered the lantern, but now, she was sure, she had even less.

Though in truth she didn't have less.

Gogo hugged Fred. "We'll figure something out, kid," she said gently.

At that small display of kindness, Fred's eyes started to water. Downer peeked over his umbrella and saw Fred's eyes watering, which made his eyes start to water as well. It's not easy to accept that your Realm is Run by a Rat who is Out of Her Mind. When Gogo saw Downer's eyes start to water, she joined right on in, too.

A Rational Number

"**H**ey, *I'm* supposed to be the saddest creature in the kingdom," the Rat said, switching to a softer tone. She stood up, shaking off some of the debris that had settled on her robe. "I'm sorry you came all this way for nothing. I do *want* to be of help. I really am trapped in this muck of sadness. There is, however, one last possibility. One way that I might be able to recover my powers and help you. Help you all."

Our friends may have felt hopeful. Or not hopeful. I can't say.

"Have you heard about the two locked boxes, each containing the other's key?" the Rat said.

"What do you mean?" Fred asked suspiciously. Why did it feel like the Rat could read her mind? Had she somehow seen her fortune?

The Rat continued: "I mean: I have a Solution to a tricky problem."

If she says the solution is A Good Night's Sleep or Knowing That You Are Loved, thought Fred, I'm going to scream.

Gogo crossed her arms. Downer set aside his umbrella.

The Rat explained: "If you can get Hart to return to me, then I'll have my powers back. But only if you can get him to return to me *of his own free will*. That's the tricky part." She held up another copy of the **Wanted: Alive or Alive** poster and shook it lightly. "I wasn't lying about this Mega-Reward.

136

I promise. When I put something on paper, I mean it. *If* you can get Hart to come back to me, then I can help you find your mom." The Rat stood up even straighter. "*If* you can get Hart to come back to me, then I can give Gogo her reward!" The Rat extended her arm out expressively. "*If* you can get Hart to come back to me, then I can help Downer to. . . ." Her arm dropped back down. "Well, sometimes I'm not sure what Downer wants . . . but I'm sure I'll be able to figure out something. What do you guys think?"

An Impossible Chapter

Gogo took out her map of The Land of Impossibility. The paper curled up into a roll, and Gogo unrolled it; then it rolled up again, and she unrolled it again. Her lockets clinked as she leaned over the map. Looking over Gogo's shoulder, Fred saw the areas labeled **No One Is Really Sure About this Part** and **Whoa, Baby** as well as a splotched section marked **The Indescribable and Poorly Defined Area Where the Fearsome Ferlings Might or Might not Dwell.** Also visible was **The High Lowlands, The Low Highlands, The Dark, Dark Wood, The Soggy Bottom** and **Here We Wish There Were Dragons.**

"I'm still waiting for an answer," the Rat said, tapping a claw. "I hate suspense!"

Downer shook his head. "We'll disappoint you if we try and fail, and we'll disappoint you if we fail to try. I'm comfortable being a disappointment. I excel at being a dis—"

"And where would we even begin looking?" Fred interrupted.

"Let me see that map," the Rat said. She put on broken reading spectacles. "Not bad, not bad. Not a bad map at all," she said. "What I know for certain is that Hart crossed over, here"—she pointed a claw—"at **The Sea of Technically True Things.** Some say Hart got lost among Ferlings on the distant shore, but that's only a rumor. I don't really know."

"I don't like the sound of searching among Ferlings," Downer said quietly.

"I'm not going to tell you there's nothing to fear from the Ferlings," the Rat said. "But they're not as bad as you imagine. The Ferlings are just . . . different. I hear they're trying to make butter out of sunshine these days. And going fishing for new clothes. Ferlings aren't fanged, or poisonous, or prone to screeching—they just don't make sense. Who am I to judge? You can see where sense has landed me," she said, gesturing around the garbage-filled room.

Fred said, "But they're fearsome, right?"

"Sure, I guess. In the sense that we fear what we don't know and don't understand. But no more beating around the bush: Are you guys going to look for my Hart and convince him to return to me, or not?"

"What strikes me," Gogo said, rolling up the map, "is that you are the Ratty Rat Rat of Reason and Rubber Boots and all. But still you failed to find Hart. Why should we expect to fare better? Does a shark expect to be invited to a guppy tea party? Does fishing in a bathtub feed a family of four?"

Downer leaned on his umbrella but did not break out into song. "Exactly. Is there any *reason* for us to expect to succeed where you have failed?"

"Of course there is," the Rat said, with mild irritation. "You have something I don't."

"Depression?" Downer asked.

"No, no," the Rat said impatiently. "I've got that, too."

"The ability to fight cobras?" Gogo inquired.

"It's unlikely that will be called upon," the Rat said with an eye roll.

"So what is it?" Downer asked.

"Maybe this won't work," the Rat said. "Isn't it obvious?!" The Rat pointed her claw at Fred. "You have her! You have the girl in the bunny slippers. You have a friend who is a . . . a child. You are a child, right? And Children Are—"

An Unwritten Chapter

Fred was finding the whole Children Are the Best Thing in the World bit increasingly . . . unsettling. Even creepy. What did Mango and Django and Argo and Ergo and Oswego and Tango and . . . and all of their brothers and sisters think? Probably they would rather be allowed to have birthday parties and grow up normally without the pressure of being The Best Things in the Entire World. She doubted those young mongeese liked everyone pointing at them, being like, *Look! There they are!*

It reminded Fred of Being the New Kid. In Fred's Unwritten Rule Book for Living, she had a Cons and Pros list about this situation:

CONS

- *Being invited to the birthday parties of kids you don't really know*
- *Not being invited to the birthday parties of kids you don't really know*
- *Wasting time worrying about what kids you don't even know think of you*
- *Wasting time worrying about what you think of kids you don't really know*
- *New teachers*

- *Feeling like a Nobody*
- *Being a Nothing*
- *Not being able to remember anyone's name*

PROS

- *Finding new places to eat lo mein noodles*

Fred was aware that her Cons and Pros list was not, strictly speaking, a Rule, but it had to go somewhere. And anyway, the Rule Book was Unwritten. It could accommodate a bit of contradiction.

This gave Fred an idea: to get Hart to return, what if they threw him a . . . B.P.? A *birthday party*! Even though that would mean disobeying Rat Rule 79? Would he attend? Maybe he would—since hadn't it been Rule 79 that had made him run away in the first place? In sum: to obey the Rat's directive to get the Hart to return might require disobeying the Rat and throwing a birthday party. Displeasing the Rat might lead to pleasing the Rat. Perhaps a Birthday Party, which was a problem, was also a Solution.

It *could* be a good plan.

She would wait to share it with her friends. She suspected (correctly) they would not approve.

Scale

After a brief huddle, the trio decided to try to find the hart. The Rat didn't wish the trio luck because, she claimed, she was rational and didn't believe in luck. But she did send them off with two very large fortune cookies. Each was about the size of a softball. "A little something to help you on your way," she said, putting the jumbo fortune cookies in an old neoprene bag she dug out of her pile of trash. Fred thought it would have been nicer if the Rat had sent them off with, say, peanut butter and pickle sandwiches, which Fred was increasingly craving. But the Rat made her own decisions. And the fortune cookies were appealing, the way that things that are the wrong size—like the spoon as tall as a giant person that Fred had once seen—are reliably so appealing. And who knew—the fortune cookies might bring them the luck the Rat claimed not to believe in.

"I'm also sending my right-hand dog to paddle you across the Sea of Technically True Things. You've met Dogma, right? Don't be afraid of him. He's all bark. I'm the one who bites."

A Sorry Chapter

"Have *you* ever met a Ferling?" Fred asked Gogo. They were heading down to the shore behind Downer, who held aloft his red umbrella like the leader of a tour.

"Honestly, no," said Gogo. "I've spent most of my life in a burrow, doing one household task after another. It was only after I lost all our family money on a Grues investment that I found myself traveling around like this, putting together odd jobs."

"A what investment?"

"*Grues.* A Grue is a very rare gem that starts off green until eventually, with the passage of time, it turns blue. So it's green . . . until it's blue . . . which is *grue.* Get it? Grues are very valuable. At least that's what the very convincing burrow-to-burrow salesman told me. I gave him everything we had." She shook her head and let out a sad laugh. "But since time has stopped, they're only a bunch of green stones that'll never turn blue."

"You mean they're emeralds."

"Nope. Just stones that are green. Once Grue gems. Now green stones. Since Rat Rule 79, their price has totally plummeted."

"They still might turn blue one day," Fred offered.

"Not unless Rule 79 is revoked. And in the history of the Rat Queen, no Rule has ever, ever been revoked. I'd say a rule-revoking is less probable than a downpour of giant pandas. Less likely than a timber wolf asking you to pass the salt."

"That seems a bit extreme, even for the Rat." Fred was beginning to hear the sound of the watery shore. "Maybe you're wrong about that."

"The Revered Rat Rule 1 is The Rat is Always Right. So you see the problem. It's the very first rule! I mean, I like some of the early rules, the more poetic ones, like Radical Rat Rule 7 about how fast light can travel, and Iridescence Rat Rule 41 about those rainbows that you can see in gasoline—that kind of stuff is great."

Gogo's words reminded Fred of her mom. "I wonder if the Rat ever tried simply apologizing to Hart."

"Apologizing for Rule 79?"

"Yeah, I guess. Or for making Hart sad, whichever." The chit-chatty sound of the seashore could now be heard. The air felt stickier.

"Funny that you mention apologizing—another name for Grues is Apology Stones." Gogo paused a moment on the trail. "Wait a moment and I'll show you." Gogo pulled a few stones out of her backpack. They were nice-looking. Smooth and creamy, as if they were made of cooled alien lava. Gogo explained, "Like, sometimes it's hard to make an apology right in the moment, when feelings are so high, but then, by the time the stone turns blue, you're ready. Grues used to be popular for that—*when this stone turns blue, know that I apologize to you*—so you could send someone a Grue stone as a way of saying, *I'm not ready to apologize yet, but I know one day I will be.* When the stone turns blue. Stepping Stones. That was another popular nickname for Grues."

"They're still pretty," Fred said. "Though of course I'm very sorry to hear that you lost all your money on them."

Gogo shrugged. She returned the stones to her backpack. "No one to blame but myself." Then, suddenly angry, she put up her fists, threatening to punch herself. "Why did you do something so stupid, Gogo?!" Sometimes a fighting spirit has nowhere to go but home. Gogo put her fists down and was calm again. "We all make decisions we regret, right?"

"Hurry up!" Downer shouted. "I may be no fun to travel with, but your presence is required."

The Technically True Chapter

The Sea of Technically True Things was bordered by a beach of chalky, white stones. A younger Fred would have tried to grind down one of the stones into what she would have believed was lemonade powder. But that Fred was gone.

"Don't take anything you hear to heart," a voice said as they neared the lapping water. "Everything they're saying is true. So don't worry about it."

It was their old not-friend Dogma speaking. Making his customary not-quite-sense.

"You're not here in relation to that ridiculous paperwork, are you?" Gogo asked suspiciously, fists up. "That would be as uncalled for as a sea urchin in a bridal bouquet. As ludicrous as a lemur at the North Pole. As—"

"Rat sent me to guide you," Dogma said. "That's what I'm going to do." Dogma still believed that the Rat was held by Ferlings—because she said she was—even if his own eyes told him she was sitting around nibbling on garbage, with no Ferlings in sight. "I help the Rat above all."

Fred bent down and gave Dogma a scratch behind the ears. "And we appreciate it," she said. She still thought Dogma was a cute little puppy, and failed to appreciate the gravity of her Time Violation.

"So you promise you're not here for—" Gogo began,

"—that silly paperwork you baselessly issued—" Downer went on,

"—to me?" Fred asked.

Dogma, who looked now even smaller than before, repeated in an even tone: "I am a whole-pizza follower of the Rat. That means I do exactly what the Rat says I should do. The Rat asked me to help guide you across the Sea of Technically True Things. I am therefore going to guide you across the Sea of Technically True Things. I recall the Time Violation of which you are not speaking, but is this a courtroom? Is this the appointed hour?" He looked around at the shore. "It is not."

He then turned his furry back on them. Using his nose, Dogma pushed out a raft that had been obscured by willow trees. Slipping, he muddied a paw and whacked his nose on the edge of the raft. He wiped his paw on some dry leaves and shook his head, wiggling his nose. He looked so gentle doing these normal, clumsy things.

As our friends boarded the raft, it wobbled and sank down a few millimeters, but remained afloat. With a long oar that he maneuvered with his front paws, Dogma pushed the wavering raft off the lemonade-stone shore. A quiet plashing attended their setting off. "I'll mention one more time: Don't take anything you hear personally," the small dog said.

The raft had two paper lanterns at the front, hanging from vertical poles at the port and starboard sides. The sky was darkening. Those round lanterns, if the stars had bothered to take notice, would have looked like a thoughtful pair of alien eyes making their way across the sea. The lanterns gave

Fred a surge of feeling, though she wasn't quite sure what
the feeling was. Or was it a Ferling?

Gogo pulled earmuffs out of her endlessly useful backpack.
"I'm used to my children criticizing me, but I'm still a bit sen-
sitive," she said in a whisper as she put the earmuffs on. "But
you still have the strength of a child. I know you'll be fine."

Now small silver fish were jumping out of the plashing
dark water. It was eerie.

"Terrestrians!" a voice called out.

"Land Denizens!"

"Earthers!"

Dogma kept on with a steady, gentle paddling.

"Oxygen snorters!" came another wobbly shout.

The raft was rocking. Fred went to stand closer to Downer,
for balance. She asked him if he was hearing what she was
hearing.

"Yes, I'm hearing it." It appeared not to bother him. "I've
got a thick skin. Mostly it's an embarrassment to have thick
skin but sometimes it's useful—"

"Leather-hides!" came a voice.

"Pedestrians!"

Fred looked around but still couldn't identify a speaker.

"It's the *Pesca Saltares*," Downer explained. "Some people
call them Jumping Fish, some call them Insult Fish. I just call
them sea life."

"Try not to mind them or talk about them, please," Dogma
said. "That makes them jumpier, and then it's more difficult
for me to steer the raft, and it's—"

"Dogmatic!" one sea-bassed out with special viciousness, followed by a loud splash.

"Talking talkers who talk!"

"What are they so angry about?" Fred asked the calm Downer.

He shrugged. "I think they get tired of people fishing for compliments."

"Two-armed mammal!" another silvery leaping voice carped.

"Hey, lay off!" Fred called out to the dark waters, cupping her hands around her mouth. "Pipe down!"

"Stay calm," Dogma said. "The raft may rock, but everything is going to be all right."

"One-nosed girl!" A splash of seawater hit Fred's face as a cold fish's dive met the water again.

"Incapable of photosynthesis!" came a voice from the left of the raft.

"Not fully grown!" came a voice from the right.

"Can't speak to bees!"

"Stop it!" Fred shouted, annoyed that she even cared.

"Ungulate!" another fish called out, with the biggest splash yet. "Landlubber!"

The raft was beginning to rock more, and Fred was getting angry. "It'll be okay," Dogma reiterated.

"Fishface!" Fred called out, lowering herself to insults. "Cold-blooded cowards!"

"Lonely!" a fish shouted back. "Introvert!"

"Ignore them," Downer said to Fred calmly.

"Easily embarrassed!" interrupted another fishy voice.

Fred leaned over the edge of the raft: "Fish for brains!" The raft nearly toppled. Dogma was catapulted into Downer's lap.

"Can you please not respond?!" Dogma begged, scrambling back to the front of the raft. The he regained his composure and said, "We're all going to be just fine."

"Cold fish!" Fred yelled, ignoring Dogma. "Pond scum eaters! Gill breathers!" Fred had more petty anger in her than she might have expected. Years of being gentle and flexible had been difficult, and left a strange residue.

Gogo's backpack got hit with an especially big splash. "All right, that's it, those fish are going to be sad as sea otters in a sandbox in about a minute here." Her fighting spirit was upon her. She took off her damp earmuffs and joined in the yelling: "Tunaverse dwellers! Jalapeño-sized appetizers!"

Now I want to interrupt these choppy waters and ask if you disliked Dogma up until this point. And even looked down on him. Not only because he's eleven inches tall and looks like he belongs in the sleeves of an emperor and there aren't even emperors anymore, but for other reasons, too. That's okay. You might think he's a bit daffy, the way he never changes his mind and follows the rules beyond the point of sense. I don't disagree with you on that. But as Gogo and Fred both kept on shouting, Dogma kept calmly repeating: "Everything is going to be okay." And reiterating: "Everything will be all right." Dogma had no factual or rational basis for what he was saying. He said it only because the Rat had said the same to him. Because he viewed it as law, as inviolable a law as the wetness of water.

"How do you know everything's going to be okay?" Fred asked.

He just knew, he said.

And it felt good to hear someone say that everything was going to be all right. The boat, with its agitated passengers and argumentative fish sidekicks, nearly capsized six or seven times. But as Dogma kept repeating his unreasonable conviction—that everything was going to be all right—the friends transitioned from insulting the Insult Fish to debating whether Dogma was right or not right. That was a more calming conversation. It was like that time that Fred dreamed that she wanted a peanut butter and pickle sandwich (on raisin bread) and first her desk turned into a sandwich, and then her bed, and then her mom, and Fred ate one sandwich after another after another after another, and, well, the dream had become a nightmare. But the point is that in the morning, after that dream-turned-nightmare, when Fred woke up, she *did* get to eat a peanut butter and pickle sandwich (on raisin bread). She ate just one. And her room and her mother were still there. What I'm saying is that in this case, Dogma was right. Everything was all right.

In relation to the raft, that is.

The Other Chapter

"**B**ananas?" a creature asked.

This was directed at Fred, who was the first off the raft. They had reached a sandy shore, with unkempt palm trees visible further inland. The island looked like a shoebox diorama Fred had once made for a book report on *Robinson Crusoe*. The sun was up. "Um, that *was* totally bananas—but how did you know?" Fred said to the creature.

"I mean: bananas or Ferlings? Everyone comes here looking for either bananas or Ferlings. Which are you looking for?"

"Oh. Ferlings, I guess? Though I have nothing against bananas." Fred took a good look at the creature before her. "We're looking for Hart"—she showed him the **Wanted: Alive or Alive** poster—"who we think might be hanging out with the Ferlings." The creature was covered in fur that glistened in the sea-light; his body was like that of a small otter; his bill was like that of a duck. He was odd. Odder than the Know-It-Owl. Odder than a unicorn.

The creature said: "I haven't seen Hart, but I'm very shy and don't get out much. I was only asking about the Ferlings because some people are afraid of Ferlings. Some people might be afraid of bananas, too. Folks have been known to be afraid of the strangest things. Some folks are even afraid of me."

"Are *you* a Ferling?" Fred asked. She peeked over her shoulder, where her friends were still talking something over with Dogma.

"No. I'm DBP. That's for Duck-Billed Platypus. Great feet, by the way."

Fred looked down and was reminded, yet again, that she was wearing her fuzzy bunny slippers.

DBP said, "Those nice feet make me think you must be a nice person. I know what it's like to be part one thing, and part another. You learn something about life when the world doesn't know what you are."

"They're old slippers, but . . . thank you? So you're not a Ferling, but do you know where they hang out? We heard Hart might be with them."

"Ferlings can turn up in the most unexpected places, it's impossible to predict. I do love them, though. They took me in when no one believed I was real."

"You mean when nobody knew what you were?"

"I mean when I couldn't get an Existence Permit."

DBP looked to Fred a bit like an animal invented in a round of the put-the-dot-in-the-squiggle game she and her mom played. "Is that what it's like here? You have to have permission to exist?"

"I'd go to the school and they'd tell me to get an Existence Permit. I'd go to the Existence Permit office and they'd tell me to bring school ID to verify my existence. Back and forth. Everyone treated me like it was *my* fault that they couldn't help me."

"But that's bananas!" Fred said sympathetically.

"Bananas? I thought you were looking for Ferlings."

"Bananas as in 'nuts.'"

"Nuts?"

"You know: cuckoo."

"Oh, yeah. Sorry. It was bananas in that way. They thought my duck bill was a mask. There were efforts to find sewing stitch marks, or safety pins. It was so embarrassing. That might be how I became so self-conscious and shy."

"That's super bananas. I'm so sorry."

"I try not to think about it. They investigated my webbed feet for falseness as well. Poke, prod, prod, poke. The Ferlings can be problematic, sure, but at least they accepted me for the duck-billed platypus I was. They didn't dissect me," DBP said.

"Here come my friends now," Fred said. "I'm sure they'd love to meet you."

Catching sight of Downer and Gogo coming up the path, DBP panicked. "*Beware the hospitalities*, I always say. I'm a shy, water-based creature at the end of the day. But thank you for listening to me. I saw those bunny feet on you and I knew you'd understand. It's nice to meet someone who understands. As for finding Hart, I wish you the best of luck. But again, *beware the hospitalities*."

And with that, DBP was back in the water, paddling her powerful duck feet and zooming away faster than Fred had imagined possible.

What Does This Chapter Look Like to You?

"**W**ell, Fred, I hope you know how to read a blot," Gogo said irritably. She held up her Topo-Illogical Map of The Land of Impossibility. It was wet from the splashes of the Insult Fish. The ink on the map had run. "All you had to do was keep your mouth closed. But you had to taunt those fish, didn't you? You had to trade insults."

Fred opened her mouth to protest, but nothing came out. Gogo was right.

"Um, didn't *you* call them jalapeño-sized?" Downer said, defending Fred by attacking Gogo.

Gogo pretended not to hear, sneezed, and took another pickle to calm herself down. Fred wondered briefly how it was that no matter how many pickles they ate, they were never out of pickles.

"Where's Dogma?" Fred said, trying to change the topic.

Looking out at the water, they saw the growing silhouette of Dogma heading away in the distance. They'd have to manage without him.

Our wayward heroes huddled around to take a closer look at the damp map. It showed purplish ink smudges of different sizes now. They squinted at it. They rotated it. Whichever way it was turned, it still looked like a bunch of blobs.

Fred spoke first: "I see what looks like a lollipop here. . . . And maybe a peanut butter and pickle sandwich over here. . . . Weird, this splotch looks like the face of my substitute teacher when my third-grade teacher got pregnant."

Around them, the palm trees did not comment. No birds chirped useful remarks.

Downer said, "I see my depressed mother. And over here, some of my less nice cousins."

Fred said, "And this scraggly zone, this looks to me like a cuckoo clock being thrown into a garbage can?"

"Uh-huh. You mean this is a total waste of time," Gogo said. "And I totally—"

"Hey, wait a minute. Look at this, guys." Downer pointed to the largest purplish blob on the map.

"A waffle?" offered Fred.

"Cotton candy that fell into a puddle?" suggested Gogo.

"I don't mean to be an optimist," Downer said, "but when I look at this, and then look at"—Downer used his trunk to point between two tall palm trees—"that . . . . You see?"

And there it was: a real-life inky purple smudge. A smudge that looked quite a bit like a tall stable door. Was it only a purplish fog that would soon dissipate? Or was it more than that?

Gogo was muttering, "So you're trying to tell me that this map somehow knew it would get wet, and had a plan for leaking into a blob shape that would match—" But then she stopped talking. She couldn't understand it, but the resemblance between the blobs was too strong to dismiss.

The purple blob in the distance didn't appear to be con-
nected to anything around it. Was it fog? An ectoplasmic
goo? A ghost in the form of architecture? As Fred stared,
it resembled a neighbor's cat, then an old xylophone from
preschool, then her mother's veined hand, and then even,
briefly, a younger Fred. It changed again, recalling a Lego
structure from Fred's past, one from which the door itself had
long been missing and only the doorframe had endured. The
doorframe was one of those weirdly un-losable Lego pieces
that stayed around, move after move, even as its companions
disappeared one by one to wherever it is that lost Lego pieces
go. Maybe to the Land of the Ferlings.

As if between a trance and a dream, Fred and her friends
walked toward the shape, whose distance from them was
difficult to estimate. It seemed to stay the same size even as
the friends walked, then jogged, and finally ran to reach it.
By the time they arrived, they were sweating and exhausted.
The shape, finally up close, had acquired a doorknob. But
the doorknob was too high to reach. Then the haze of the
shape dissipated. The panting travelers could make out
many creatures, which looked like . . . well . . . locomoting
inkblots. As with the initial blot, it was hard to describe
them. They were all different, and yet they shared a distinct
non-distinctness. A non-distinctness that was both waxy and
woolly. Frumptious and froolly. These blots looked ready
for wind and rain, for whatever weather might reach them.
Or they might melt away in a moment. The blots also all
had short stick legs and wore sneakers. That was their one

highly recognizable aspect. Were they a child's drawings of dark sheep?

Whatever they were, Fred thought, they were definitely not the Fantastically Fearsome Ferlings.

That is what Fred thought. But that was not the case.

Chapter Ate

These Ferlings lived in a very strange, very rare, very eerie landscape that was part desert, part jungle, and part tundra—a desungdra. Cacti stood in patches of snow. A green grove of bamboo sprouted from red sand dunes. Orchids blossomed out of a rocky steppe. A cluster of raspberry bushes grew inside a dried-up wadi. Gone was the sandy shore.

Downer hushed a little song:

> *Oh Ferlings of fevers*
> *And frightful furry feelings*
> *Daffo-dill-pickles*
> *And funny filaments*
> *They may be less than fulsome—*

A blob approached our group of friends. "Do you come bearing gifts?" the blob asked.

Another blob approached. And then another. And then another and another and another, quickly encircling our trio. The Ferlings seemed to be growing taller, and messier.

Gogo raised her fists. "I'm warning you. No one touches these lockets."

"No gifts?" the initial Ferling said.

Downer's ears drooped. He said, "I'm sorry. We've let you down. We've failed. I apologize."

The Ferlings blobbily wavered and trembled and mumbled and muffled as they drew nearer and nearer.

"Why no gifts?"

"Are you guests?"

"We love gifts."

"We love guests."

It was spooky, the shadowy mumbling.

Then Fred had a thought.

Reaching into Gogo's backpack, she pulled out one of the two giant cookies the Rat had given her. With a formal flourish, as if at a royal court, Fred held the cookie in the palm of her hand and presented it to the Ferlings.

The cookie looked goofy like that, it must be said. Just like you'd expect an oversized fortune cookie to look.

But the Fearsome Ferlings oohed and aahed over it as if it were a precious object. One of the smaller Ferlings caressed the cookie; others crowded around it in awe. Finally a tray was produced and the cookie was carefully placed on it. "We'll plant this," one of the Fearsome Ferlings said. "We've always wanted a cookie tree."

Fred decided not to tell them that cookies don't, technically, grow on trees. Instead she said, "Um, I don't know for sure if that will work."

"Of course you don't know," a tall Ferling said in a cheery voice. "You're too nice to know."

A smaller Ferling walked away with the cookie on the tray, followed by a larger Ferling carrying a shovel.

"Can I offer you a lemonade?" a broad Ferling said to

Fred. "With a paper umbrella? And pink ice cubes? We love guests."

"Sure," Fred said. She loved paper umbrellas.

Downer was led to a lounge chair and offered a tray of dumplings. He loved dumplings.

Gogo was set up on a satiny pillow and given a plate of chocolate coins wrapped in gold foil. Yep—she loved gold chocolate coins.

Naturally, our friends were wondering what was so very fearsome about these very friendly Ferlings. They seemed positively fantastic. Once you got used to them. Fred found herself reclining on a marshmallowy sofa with a delicious lemonade. She could not have been more comfortable. Gogo, who somehow was far away, was showing her lockets one by one to other Ferlings, who cooed and giggled with delight. Downer, even farther away, had Ferlings fanning him as he fed on more and more, and bigger and bigger dumplings. In fact, Fred found it difficult to tell the Ferlings apart from the dumplings, especially as Downer was drifting still farther away. As was Gogo—and the Ferlings looking at her lockets seemed to be shrinking and turning into locket-sized Ferlings.

Everybody and everything was becoming blurrier and farther away and more alike.

Fred grew uneasy.

A nearby Ferling inquired: "Would you like some water to wash your feet? How about the toy car you wanted so much when you were five? A gingerbread house that doesn't fall apart at the frosting seams? With gumdrops that don't taste like soap?"

Beware the hospitalities, the duck-billed platypus had said.

Fred's bunny slipper feet usually made her feel childish and semi-embarrassed, but now they gave Fred courage. She knew what she wanted. And it wasn't a lemonade with a paper umbrella or even a peanut butter and pickle sandwich. What she wanted was to find the hart. Find Hart and talk him into coming to a birthday party that she hoped the Rat would attend as well. And then—well, that remained to be seen.

Fred spoke up. "I don't want any of *those* things, thank you," she said. "But there is something I *would* like."

"Go ahead."

"I'm trying to deliver a very important party invitation—"

"We love parties!"

"Um, the party isn't for you—"

"Oh—"

"Though of course you would be very welcome to attend. Gogo has the invitations in her backpack. But first we need to track down the guest of honor, a deer named Hart—"

"Yes, yes, lovely."

Fred thought she could make out Gogo in the distance, having a head massage. Downer was trying to reach a cherry at the bottom of his cola. Both of them looked even smudgier and more incorrectly sized than before. As if water had spilled on them, and their ink was running. Reaching into her pocket, she retrieved the **Wanted: Alive or Alive** poster. "Do you know this deer?"

"Would you like a second lemonade?" the Ferling nearest to Fred asked, ignoring the **Wanted** poster. "This time with a striped silly crazy loop straw? Or a peanut butter and pickle sandwich. Would you like that? I have a feeling you would like that."

"Did you hear me? Do you know this deer?"

The Ferlings fell silent.

"I need to reach this deer, Hart, to let him know about the party in his honor," Fred said, adding quickly, "It'll be a really fun party, you guys will love it. I heard Hart was hanging out with you guys. Do you know where I could find him?"

One Ferling coughed politely. "We don't know."

Another laughed and said, "Who said we would know?"

"The Rat said so," said Fred.

No response.

"And the Rat is never wrong. Or so I've been told."

No response.

"You know, the Ratty-Rat-Rat of Railways and Running Long Jumps, and—"

The largest Ferling spoke: "We do not know the Rat."

"You don't?"

"And we do not know the deer."

"You don't?"

"We don't know anything. We work hard to keep it that way. We are against knowing. Whatever you're talking about is a no-know, as far as we're concerned."

"You guys *are* Ferlings, right?"

"I don't know," one inky-blot Ferling said. "Any of you guys know?" He was addressing a group of other inky-blot Ferlings. They were all starting to look alike again in their differences.

"Nope."

"No."

"Definitely no."

"We don't know anything, not even the backs of our hands."

"We certainly don't know which side our bread is buttered on."

"Excuse me?" asked our bunny-slippered heroine.

"What you don't know can't hurt you."

"That's why we prefer the devil we don't know to the devil we do."

"Wait, what?" the wise not-quite-child asked.

"Other creatures are dying to know stuff."

"We don't want to die and so we don't want to know."

"And we certainly don't like it when other people stick their knows in our business."

The Ferlings were all still standing around, hospitably. Or hostilely. It was difficult to tell the difference. Fred looked around to see her friends. Was that large inky grey blot holding Downer's red umbrella? Where was Gogo? She thought she could hear the clinking of lockets but could spy no mongoose. Fred's heart began to beat very quickly.

"Where are my friends?" she asked in a panic.

"How would we know?" said a Ferling voice. Or was it the voices of many Ferlings? Their numbers had increased. They were getting closer and closer again, chattering about lemonade and pickles and purple socks. . . .

Beware of the hospitalities. If Fred didn't escape soon, would she become one of them? She looked at her bunny slippers for strength.

And had an idea. "I know," she said, out loud—out loudly, you could say.

The Ferlings froze.

Fred hopped up from the marshmallowy chair. "If *I* know something for sure," she declared, "and I tell you what it is that I know, then *you'll* know it."

"Not so fast," a Ferling said. "People often think they know things but actually don't. Kids especially." Ferling laughter filled the air.

"I know that I'm loved," Fred said triumphantly.

The Ferlings gasped, became very blobby indeed, and with a wail scattered into the desungdra.

The Empty Set

In the distance, Fred spied a red brick building. On it was written **The School of** . . . of something. . . . The words were partially obscured by climbing vines. She could no longer see any Ferlings. Nor any friends. Where could they be? Fred's mom taught in a school. Or often did. It's a long shot, thought Fred, but you never know—her mom might have taken yet another job at yet another location. Maybe this red school building was that location. Might her mom be teaching here, at the School of . . . Something . . . and hadn't yet found the courage to tell Fred about the move?

Through a ground-floor window, Fred saw a classroom. An ordinary classroom. Or so it first appeared. Her mom was *not* in the classroom, she quickly ascertained. But a badger was there, standing near a clean chalkboard at the front of the room. If someone in this Land of Impossibility knows something, Fred said to herself, I bet that person—or creature—is here, at school.

She saw no door, so Fred climbed in through the window, her slippered foot knocking a book from the sill. The book landed with a smack and fell open to a blank page. Fred picked up the book. A quick inspection revealed that all the pages were blank. Fred set the blank book gently back on the sill.

She took a seat at the back of the classroom, between a penguin who didn't seem to know that this was totally the wrong weather for a penguin, and a koala whose eyes were heavy and tired. Neither creature acknowledged Fred. Neither seemed to be paying attention to the badger teacher, either. The penguin quietly drummed his feathery flippers; the koala chewed slowly on eucalyptus leaves. Which smelled so nice.

Fred heard a very small voice singing.

Foxes sleep in the forest
Lions sleep in their dens
Goats sleep on the mountaintops. . . .

It was a tune at once sweet and melancholy, like one of those lullabies that made Fred cry when she was little even though they were supposed to make her feel good. Autumn lullabies, she called them. There was a mouse on Fred's desk. The mouse was folding tiny laundry as he sang.

"What a pretty song," Fred said quietly to the laundry-folding mouse.

"I'm not singing!" claimed the mouse with a tiny shout.

"Okay," whispered Fred. "No problem."

The mouse returned to folding the clothes, which were very little, even for a mouse.

As if he'd read Fred's mind, the mouse said, "I'm saving these clothes for when I'm small again."

Normally—even only yesterday—Fred would have told the mouse that you don't grow smaller. But now she didn't say that. She let it go. "I like that shirt with the elephant on it," she said.

The mouse held it up so they could both have a better look at it. "Don't you think I must have been so cute when I was small?"

Fred laughed, quietly. She was in a classroom after all. "You're still small. You're still cute."

"You don't understand," the mouse said. "I used to be amazing."

"Sure," said Fred.

"I was! I was amazing. I would say 'up' and 'burrito' and 'in the distance' and my family would clap and laugh." Tears appeared in the mouse's eyes.

"You can still say those things," Fred said. "You just said them."

"It's not the same," the mouse said with a sigh. "Back then my mom was amazed at my having eight fingers and ten toes."

Eight was a surprising number for fingers, but Fred looked and saw that the mouse indeed had eight. "You still have those things," Fred said to the mouse. "You still have eight fingers. You still have ten toes. And they're great."

Now the mouse was really snuffling, and wiping his nose on his clean little T-shirt. In a mouse-loud voice, he barked, "You don't understand! It's not the same!"

"WHAT'S GOING ON BACK THERE?" boomed the badger from the front of the classroom.

"I don't know, sir!" called out the penguin nervously.

"Correct," said the badger, relaxing again. "Excellent."

RIVKA GALCHEN

The koala continued chewing on the fragrant eucalyptus leaves, now staring at a spot on the wall.

The mouse frowned at Fred and went back to folding his tiny laundry.

Fred raised her hand. Respectfully. Perhaps too respectfully, because the badger ignored her. "Excuse me, I have a question," she called out politely.

"Wrong!" the badger called out. Then: "Can someone explain to the new student the rule that no questions are allowed?"

"Yes, sir!" said the penguin, koala, and mouse in unison.

"But you just asked a question," Fred said to the badger, annoyed.

"Did I?" barked the badger.

"No, Sir!" the students said in unison again, then promptly returned to being spaced out.

Fred began, "Is there any—"

"One more question from you and we'll have to get out the Quiet Bug. I should warn you that her bite is quite itchy. Or so they say. I myself have unlearned that."

174

Interrogative
Chapter

If you're going to rob a bank, don't get a speeding ticket on the way there. Fred read that in a book for adults once, and it struck her as useful information.

Therefore Fred did not violate the badger's rule against asking questions—because soon she would be violating a bigger rule.

That a plan to throw a birthday party for a deer was equivalent to robbing a bank in this analogy was, she thought, just one of the disheartening, doolally, and downright disgraceful consequences of The Essential and Very Good and No One Can Disagree with Rat Rule 79. Whatever. Fred could adjust to a new situation.

She said to the badger, "I imagine you have an interesting story to tell."

The other students' studious boredom was ruffled. There was some curious mumbling. The mouse stopped folding his laundry.

"What did you say?" the badger said.

Fred refrained from pointing out that once again the badger was asking a question. "I said: I imagine you have an interesting story to tell."

Perhaps the badger was weakened by vanity. Or by a longing to be asked to tell his story, a longing never fulfilled since he forbade asking questions of any kind. Either way, Badger cleared his throat.

"Mine is a glorious story," he began, unconvincingly. "One sunny Friday morning, a Ferling approached me and said, 'You are the wisest of all wolverines.' I was offended. For starters, I'm a badger and not a wolverine. But also because I felt pretty sure that I knew Nothing, or close enough to Nothing, and I had worked so hard to get to that point. And here was this Ferling accusing me of being wise. Do you have any idea how hard it is to not know anything? Of course you don't. How would you know?"

"Yes, sir!" Penguin said randomly.

"Maybe the Ferling mistook you for someone else," Fred suggested. "A wolverine, for example."

Badger said, "He knew exactly who I was. In his way. And I realized that the Ferling was telling me I was the wisest *because I knew the least.* That's when I decided my mission in life was to pass on to the next generation everything I didn't know. To teach our youngsters Nothing. I would become the best Know-Nothing I could be, and I would help others unlearn as I had."

This Know-Nothing Badger reminded Fred of the Know-It-Owl—they were both so annoyingly sure of themselves! She said, "But you just admitted that you *knew* that you *know* nothing. So that was something you knew."

"I'm not perfect," the badger admitted, "but I definitely know less than your mother. Your mother knows way too much—"

"My mom? What do you know about my mom?" Fred asked impulsively, breaking her resolution not to violate the badger's rule.

"No questions!" shouted the Badger.

"You said she knows too much."

"I said no such thing."

"Why are you talking about her? Is she here?"

"Questions, questions. You're probably already thirteen years old. Soon you won't even be a child anymore."

Reminded of her birthday, Fred lit up with a fury she didn't quite understand. She recalled her mom once saying to her, *The younger you are, the more important you are.* Her mom must have meant it in a nice way. Or even in a not-serious way. *But that means growing up is terrible,* Fred had said. Her mom replied, *No, because there's an upside. The upside to getting older is that you keep learning.* Fred found the exchange annoying, and disturbing.

"Do you know which way is up?" Fred asked the badger, with an angry edge to her voice.

"Cease with the questions, please."

"Do you know what koalas eat?" she asked, pointing at her peer, who was nibbling away.

"Stop."

"You do know. You do know which way is up. And what koalas eat."

"Vile accusation!"

"You even know where the hart is, don't you? I bet Hart even attended your silly school."

"Now you're really badgering me—"

A deer was pressing his face to the classroom window. Fred didn't notice. Neither did the badger. But perhaps a part of them did. Fred found herself feeling a wave of compassion for the pompous Know-Nothing Badger. And the badger found himself feeling a wave of compassion for the knows-y girl.

The deer, who surely we know was Hart, moved away from the window.

Chapter Grue

"I'm sorry for how I was earlier," Badger said to Fred. "I apologize."

"I'm sorry, too," Fred said. "For being so rough like that."

Badger took a seat, like his pupils. "We've been through some trying times, here at the school. It wasn't always so . . . so . . . so *blah* like this. When the Rat and Hart were still a family, this was a glorious place. They used to come visit here together. Just as Rat and Hart were together, Learning and Unlearning were together. Rat would actually have her B.P.s here, if you can believe it. With cake and turning off the lights and those candles glimmering in everyone's faces. It seems hard to imagine now how the Ratty Rat of Rationality and Rubik's Cubes and Refractors would ever value a School of Unlearning, but in those times, she saw unlearning as *the basis* of learning. She would come here with Hart, and Rat would show Hart an umbrella and ask: What is this? Hart would say: a portable roof! Because, you see, Hart was so young he didn't know what an umbrella was. But of course not knowing what an umbrella was meant he could see something the rest of us couldn't. Creatures came to this school calling the sea 'the sea,' but they left calling it the Dolphin Road or the Big Dark Flat or even the Wild Big See. It was here that our ancestors first unlearned that the sun revolved around the earth. It was here they forgot to think of themselves as much different from monkeys, even from fish. That the Rat Queen herself often visited the school was one reason students trusted us. But ever since The Essential and Very Good and No One Can Disagree with Rat Rule 79, this place no longer makes sense *or* nonsense. Before Rat Rule 79, this school was the very night-light of truth. Now? Kaput. Plain old darkness reigns."

Fred noticed the badger's dark eyes, the earnest white stripe on his head. She remembered that badger babies, unlike many wild animals, are born blind and with almost no fur. Vulnerable and huddling, they struggle and grow, leaving the den for the first time only after months of staying home. But once they leave, they live mostly solitary lives. Fred wanted to hug the badger. She ventured, "If I can convince Hart to talk to the Rat again, things might return to what they were before."

The badger shrugged. "I doubt it."

"Where is Hart?"

"I can't answer your questions," said Badger. "I don't mean that in an unkind way. It's simply not who I am."

"Okay. I understand. Thank you, at least, for talking with me. I won't ask you any more questions. But I do want to say that one day soon there might be . . . well . . . a gathering . . . of baked goods and friends. One that takes a non-tragic view of the earth having completed another revolution around the sun. Right now the invitations are in my friend's backpack. I'll send you one. If I can find my friends. I have to go now, to look for them, though I don't know where they'll be."

As Fred turned to leave, Badger called out to our slippered heroine. "I admit I know at least one thing. What I know is that if there's something you really want to know—and it sounds like there are a few things—you should pass through the Nothing Room. And after that, through the more daunting Nearly Nothing Room. I know this advice coming from a tired old badger doesn't sound like much. But no matter who or what or when you're looking for: visiting those places will bring you closer to knowing than you were before." The badger looked around anxiously for a moment. "I don't go there anymore. But when I was a child, I did. I had more courage then."

The badger pointed to a sign on the wall: **The Nothing Room.** The sign bore an arrow that looked like the solution to Fred's mom's nine-dot puzzle. That arrow pointed down a dark hallway, whose end could not be seen.

Nobody's Chapter

Fred was nervous about walking down the hallway without first going back to find Downer and Gogo among the Ferlings. But something about the uncanny familiarity of the arrow on the sign—well, it seemed like it should be obeyed. And the sign was merely directing her down a hallway. No big deal, right?

The hallway was lit with dim, ineffective bulbs that crackled quietly. White paint footprints decorated the floor. After walking and walking, she wasn't sure how far, Fred came upon a black door with an old-fashioned glass doorknob.

She opened the door cautiously, as if it might lead to nowhere.

A lone figure sat on a stool in an otherwise unfurnished room.

"Oh, hey," said Fred. "Sorry to interrupt. I thought nobody would be here."

"That's correct," the figure said kindly. "I'm Nobody."

Fred hesitated, her hand still on the doorknob. It was very difficult to say what Nobody looked like. Nobody looked a bit like pretty much everyone Fred had ever known.

"Come on in," Nobody said. "There's plenty of Nothing to go around." In front of Nobody was a large blank canvas. "Maybe you can help me. I've been trying to paint something that's not here."

Fred stepped inside. "Something from your imagination?" The door closed behind her, then vanished. Everywhere was equally lit, and the source of the light was nowhere to be seen.

Nobody laughed. "Oh no. Once I imagine something, it's in here," Nobody said, pointing to Nobody's noggin. "It's no longer *not* here. Unless you consider the imagination not to be a real thing, which it is. So you see the problem."

"Um, I *almost* see the problem." Fred was longing for the scent of the koala's eucalyptus leaves again. Or hay. Here there was precisely no smell.

"Make yourself at home, please," Nobody said.

There was nowhere to sit. Fred started to shiver. It was cold in the Nothing room, and weirdly lonely being with Nobody. Though Nobody seemed as nice as anybody else. "It's a bit scary in here," Fred said. Which was pretty brave of her to admit. "Or scary isn't quite the right word, but I feel further away from home than I've ever felt in my life."

"I get it," Nobody said. "I know how you feel. Nobody knows how *everybody* feels," Nobody said. "Though lately, no one seems to want anyone to know how they feel, not even me! Thank you for coming to talk to me. So many people used to come here, to tell me how they felt, so that Nobody would know. I heard people's hopes, fears, secrets. It was a difficult job, but also an interesting one. But since The Essential and Very Good and No One Can Disagree with Rat Rule 79, everything has changed. When even the simple private act of getting older is illegal, everyone feels like a criminal all the time. You see the problem? That's my guess, anyway. I do think people would feel better if they talked to me about it. They may be afraid." Nobody looked lost in thought, or in a dream.

"I'm sorry to hear that," Fred said. Then: "I'm Fred, by the way. I forgot to introduce myself."

"Very nice to meet you," Nobody said, quite sadly.

"How long have you been working on this painting?" Fred asked, hoping to cheer Nobody up.

Nobody shrugged. "That's hard to say. For most of my life, I made good old-fashioned Nothing. You know Swiss cheese—I made those holes. I made the empty spaces in the nets the fishermen use on the Sea of Technically True Things. I did the cavities in English muffins. The air pockets in crunchy chocolate bars—also my handiwork. But nowadays so few people want Nothing; nearly everybody wants Something. I still do some donuts, of course. Every donut needs a hole."

"Those are wonderful things you do," Fred said.

Nobody smiled. "You're on a mission, aren't you?"

"How did you know?"

"It's very obvious. You're full of heart. That was nice of you, by the way, asking me about my work. Turns out even I need someone to talk to! Anyhow, I can point out the way for your mission."

"You can?"

"Yep. The next step in your journey won't be easy, but remember as you go on to the Nearly Nothing room: Nobody has faith in you. I really do."

A dark gap, like a tunnel entrance, appeared at the center of Nobody's painting of Nothing.

Fred thanked Nobody for Nobody's time.

"It's nothing," he said. "Thank *you*. Now go on."

Googol and Other Plexes

Different languages have various special words for extraordinarily high numbers, and for exceptionally low numbers. In English you can talk about Novemdecillions, about Quinquagintacentillions, even about Graham's number. An n-plex is 10^n and you can make n as big as you please, or you can also make n-minexes of 10^{-n} to get in the neighborhood of assorted tiny-nesses, and jiffies, and Furmans. These are fun words, all of them. But they're also straightforward ones. In Japanese, a 56-plex is called *kougasha*. *Kougasha* translates roughly as "sands of the Ganges." An 80-plex is called *fukashigi*, which means "don't even think about it." The littlest numbers have poetic names, too. A 16-minex is called *shunsoku*—"breathing instant." And 23-minex, or *jou*, translates into "clean."

Next to Nothing

Fred found herself crawling through a long dark tunnel, which twinkled here and there, like a very near night sky. As she crawled along, thoughts came to her mind that didn't quite feel like *her* thoughts. Yet there they were, in her head. And they kept coming. "There are diamonds in the sea of Uranus," a thought said. Which I am told is true. "A million earths can fit into the sun," came next. Did Fred even know that? Now she did. "The sun is a medium-sized star tucked in an unremarkable arm of an average-sized galaxy that one particular life form terms the Milky Way," came another so-called thought. "When the sun enters into its red dwarf phase, earth will crash into the sun, *or* the sun will burn off all the water in earth's seas." These "thoughts" made Fred feel small, yet they also charmed her. She wore planet pajamas for a reason. She was a girl who had once known the names of the moons of Saturn.

The thoughts, however, didn't merely keep coming. They started escalating. "For every human being, there are 19 million shrimp!" It was as if the thoughts were thinking her, instead of the other way around. "The moon is 22 nilli-trillion times the size of your heart," said the next thought. "All the stars you can see in the darkest sky are a fraction of a fraction of a fraction of a fraction of a fraction of a fraction of the extremely and very teeny-tiny fraction of the universe's stars in your galaxy." Fred's near-nothingness was beginning to get to her now. "Mosquitoes will outlive humanity by 4.1 billion years."

I'm going to stop there. Fred has considerably more courage than I do. I won't share the escalations through which she passed. I myself feel close enough to nothing already. Let's just say that a few yards further into that tunnel, Fred felt lower than a snake's belly, then lower than chewed gum on a snake's belly, then lower than a grain of dirt on chewed gum on a snake's belly, then lower than a silicon molecule in a grain of dirt on chewed gum on a snake's belly, and so on and so on.

Fred's Lemma Chapter

L ong ago, it was believed that lemmings rained down from the heavens in the spring and then *faded*, like flowers, once it grew cold. After all, these cute little furry creatures were visible in the summertime and then disappeared without a trace, around the same time as flowers did. Eventually it was discovered that lemmings didn't fade: hordes of them were observed jumping to their deaths off steep seaside cliffs in Norway. *Sheesh*, people must have thought.

But lemmings don't jump to their deaths.

What few people know is that lemmings can swim. They jump into the sea in order to migrate from one feeding place to another.

Square Two

When Fred emerged from the Nearly Nothing Tunnel, Gogo and Downer ran up to her like two birders coming upon the extinct dodo. Or like sailors starved of Vitamin C coming upon an orange grove. Gogo and Downer thought Fred was considerably more than nearly nothing. They thought she was really quite something. She felt the same way about them. Quite a lot of hugging went on. I'm not saying there was more hugging than there are shrimp in the sea, but still, a lot.

"But how did you guys escape from the Ferlings?" Fred asked.

"I nodded off!" Downer announced proudly. "I dreamed about losing my umbrella. Which was devastating. I woke up from that dream in such a panic that nothing the Ferlings offered could distract me." Downer opened and closed his umbrella, then put it away again, smiling.

Gogo explained, "I was unwrapping yet another gold-foil-covered chocolate coin. The gold foil started to look like my lockets. Then I saw the face of Bingo impressed on the chocolate of one of the coins. Next the face of Argo. Then Django. And I can tell you: it was terrifying. I didn't want to eat my kids! Even though they're cute as pie, of course. I was out of there as fast as a prairie dog in a foxhole."

Fred said, "We may be back at square one when it comes

to finding Hart. But square one looks a lot better to me than it did before."

"Hang on a minute," Gogo said. "As I skedaddled from the Ferlings I had a thought. Let me show you." She unrolled her topo-illogical map and pointed to **The Dark, Dark Wood**. "Deer love the woods, right? And my children talk about a working clocktower in those woods. It might be a fairy tale. But the children tell stories of a place where time still ticks, where, you know, B.P.s still happen. Where there are peanut butter sandwiches, and presents, and games—the whole dream. Like a big rock candy mountain, though I don't see one marked on this map. Who knows if any of it's true, but maybe we should look for Hart there?"

Fred scanned the horizon, looking for the Dark, Dark Wood.

Downer said, "The worst that happens is that we fail. Which I am used to."

In the distance, Fred made out glowing orbs, bouncing along the ground like hopping cranes. The orbs shone like neon highlighter pens, in yellow, green, orange, and pink. Fred pointed.

"Oh," Downer said, suddenly dejected. "Those are the Round Tuits."

"They're what-to-its?" asked Fred.

"Round Tuits!" Downer repeated.

"Gives me the heebie-jeebies," Gogo said.

"We don't want them to catch up with us," Downer said.

They were beautiful, there in the distance. They looked like the lint balls you might get if you tossed a sunrise into a dryer.

Fred turned away from the eerie and beautiful Tuits, and back to the splotchy blot on the topo-illogical map that marked **The Dark, Dark Wood**. She felt uneasy, yet determined.

"Let's try," said Fred, nervously. "We may as well try."

The Perilous
Querulous Chapter

The way to the Dark, Dark Wood took them through a field of winter wheat. Then across some marshy hills that emerged onto gravelly scree. They passed some rocky crags, then trudged through a series of chilly slot canyons. As the landscape changed, so did the moods of the adventurers.

"I think the Rat might also be my mom," Fred confided to Gogo, who was proceeding quickly, nervously.

"You think your mom is a childish and powerful rodent who eats aluminum cans?" Gogo asked, consulting the half-ruined map as she walked. "That's exactly what I worry my children must be thinking about me."

"It's not that," Fred said glumly. "Maybe it was what the Rat was wearing."

"Maybe you're the Rat," Gogo snapped.

"Maybe," said Fred, quietly. "Maybe I'm a ratty little beast." She wiped a tear from her face. Her pace slowed, and she fell back in step with Downer. "I feel so down in the dumps," Fred said to the sad elephant.

"That's because we're in The Dumps," Downer explained calmly, pointing out the black-rocked walls of the slot canyon through which they were making their way. "It looks like it has no end, but it has one, I promise. I've been here before."

The slot canyon eventually opened out onto a field of purple flowers. A mesmerizing field. Infuriatingly bright. With a pink-lemonade scent.

"You walk so LOUDLY," Fred complained to Downer.

"Gogo's walk is way too bouncy," Downer moaned. "It's making me dizzy, just looking at it."

"Hair is weird," Gogo said to Fred. "What do you have against fur?"

"You're quick to pick a fight," Fred retaliated.

"You need to pick up the pace," Gogo told Fred.

"Both of you need to pipe down," Downer said, "Pipe down and buck up and—"

Dear reader, have you ever heard of Purple Tantrums? That field was filled with Purple Tantrum flowers; the lemonade scent was from the Tantrum dander.

Gogo started sneezing. Downer started scratching an itch that didn't exist.

And for some reason Fred, even though she was a very clever girl, decided that now, when everyone was at their most irritable, was the right moment to share with her friends her not exactly perfect birthday-party plan. Not only that, she was annoyed with them that they didn't already know about it.

Gogo responded, "I live with seventeen small mongeese who have to be reminded not to eat pennies, and I still think that this is the worst, most terrible, and extraordinarily unwise idea I have heard in a long, long, long, long, long, long time. Maybe ever."

Downer felt no differently: "You think a 103-year prison sentence and a gazillion-dollar fine aren't enough to have hanging over your head already?"

"And what about *our* heads?" Gogo complained. We'll be seen as your accomplices."

"It's like you don't even care about us."

"This is just the kind of bananas thing that a human would come up with. Cold-blooded rattlesnakes with three-chambered hearts have more heart than you," said Gogo.

"*Everyone* loves B.P.s," Fred insisted, gathering up a bouquet of the tantrums.

"I don't," said Downer.

Fred said: "Everybody but grouches, cowards, and—"

Downer interrupted: "This idea is about as good as mustard cupcakes—"

Gogo agreed: "Or cat-litter confetti—"

"Or pin-the-tail on the balloon—"

chapter e

When our friends finally made it out of the field of Purple Tantrums and reached the edge of the Dark, Dark Wood—a Cuckoo Clock Tower spire poking out above the trees—they were exhausted, regretful, and hungry. The sky had grown dark. No Round Tuit orbs could be spied anywhere. Gogo dug around in her very useful backpack, out of which she produced a single container of instant ramen noodles. "I was given this by the Ferlings. For all I know, it's a packet of shoelaces, but I don't think I can bear another pickle."

Fred examined the container. It looked like one of those single servings of ramen that she sometimes made for herself as an afternoon snack. The label read, "Irrational Noodle Love. Servings per container: ∞."

Irrational is a weird word. Not only because of those rs and the way it sounds like *eerie*. Sometimes "irrational" means thinking outside the rules of reason. Sometimes it means numbers that can't be written as a fraction and that, when you write them out as decimals, go on and on and on and on and on, forever. Like, for example, the number: 2.71828182 84590452353602874713526624977572470936999595 74966967627724076630353547594571382178525166427427466391932003059921817413596629043572900334295260595630738132328627943490763233

8298807531952510190115738341879307021540891
4993488416750924476146066808226480016847741
1853742345442437107539077744992069551702761
8386062613313845830007520449338265602976067
3711320070932870912744374704723069697720931
0141692836819025515108657463772111252389784
4250569536967707854499699679468644549059879
3163688923009879312773617821542499922957635
1482208269895193668033182528869398496465105
8209392398294887933203625094431173012381970
6841614039701983767932068328237646480429531
1802328782509819455815301756717361332069811
2509961818815930416903515988885193458072738
6673858942287922849989208680582574927961048
4198444363463244968487560233624827041978623
2090021609902353043699418491463140934317381
4364054625315209618369088870701676839642437
8140592714563549061303107208510383750510115
7477041718986106873969655212671546889570350
3540212340784981933432106817012100562788023
5193033224745015853904730419957777093503660
4169973297250886876966403555707162268447162
5607988265178713419512466520103059212366771
9432527867539855894489697096409754591856956
3802363701621120477427228364896134225164450
7818244235294863637214174023889344124796357
4370263755294448337998016125492278509257782
2562092622648326277933386566481627725166401

9105900491644998289315056604725802778631 86
4155195653244258698294695930801915298721 17
2556347546396447910145904090586298496791 28
7406870504895858671747985466775757320568 12
8845920541334053922000113786300945560688 16
6740016984205580403363795376452030402432 25
6613527836951177883863874439662532249850 65
4995886234281899707733276171783928034946 501
4345588970719425863987727547109629537415 211
1513683506275260232648472870392076431005 958
4116612054529703023647254929666938115137 322
7536450988890313602057248176585118063036 442
8123149655070475102544650117272115551948 668
5080036853228183152196003735625279449515 828
4188294787610852639813955990067376482922 443
7528718462457803619298197139914756448826 260
3903381441823262515097482798777996437308 997
0388867782271383605772978824125611907176 639
4650706330452795466185509666618566470971 134
4474016070462621568071748187784437143698 821
8559670959102596862002353718588748569652 200
0503117343920732113908032936344797273559 552
7734907178379342163701205005451326383544 000
1863239914907054797780566978533580489669 062
9511943247309958765523681285904138324116 072
2602998330535370876138939639177957454016 137
2236187893652605381558415871869255386061 647
79834025435128....

And that is only the very beginning of this particular irrational number.

"Is there enough?" Downer asked. "I'm as hungry as an elephant."

"If the Servings per Container is correct," Fred said doubtfully, "there's enough Noodle Love for all of us and more." That 8 lying down on its side, Fred remembered, meant infinity.

Gogo found a camp kettle for boiling water in her backpack, along with some bowls and a serving fork. Downer built a small campfire. Once the water boiled, the noodles cooked in three minutes. Fred forked out noodles to each of her friends. No matter how many noodles she forked out of that small container, there were always plenty more. As the friends slurped on the noodles, the purple feelings of the tantrums faded to a shy pink. No additional harsh words were exchanged. Noodles are delicious and deserve all of one's attention.

"Maybe what you were saying isn't such a bad idea," Gogo said to Fred gently. "About throwing a B.P. I'm sorry I was so rude back there. I just think that throwing a B.P., well . . . it's risky."

Fred slurped some noodles. "I agree. It is risky. And I don't even know how to invite the hart. He can't come to a party he doesn't even know about. It's probably a dumb idea."

"It's not like we have a better idea," Downer conceded.

"I wonder if it would be better if we surprised them," Gogo said. "We could tell the Rat it was for the Hart, and tell Hart it was for the Rat—"

"Or tell both of them that it was for me?" Fred suggested. "Since I'm not from here, maybe that would somehow make it okay."

"I wonder if everyone's too out of practice to even come to a B.P.," said Gogo.

"Or too shy," said Downer.

As the friends talked it over, a small deer (who really wasn't so small—he was only in the distance) emerged at the edge of the clearing where they sat.

"Look," Fred said. "What a sweet little deer."

"I would say that's more a medium-sized deer than a little deer," corrected Downer.

"I would go with large," Gogo said. "But that may just be me."

Hesitantly, the deer approached the campfire.

"We have plenty," Gogo said to the deer, now that the mellow mood had wholly overtaken her. "Enough to feed a convention of condors, a hungry reunion of hippopotami. Join us. Unless you want to fight; I could do that, too. Though I'm enjoying my noodles."

The deer quietly took a seat near them, and Fred offered the deer a bowl. "Wow," said the deer, accepting the bowl. "It's so long since I've had Irrational Love Noodles. Thank you."

The stars above were beginning to brighten.

"Would you say most creatures like parties?" Fred asked the deer. "We were talking about throwing a party."

"I'm more of a quiet chat around the campfire kind of guy," the deer said. "But that's me."

"Hmm. Well, we don't even know how to distribute invitations," Fred laughed.

"Or make party hats," added Gogo.

"Or prepare tasty snacks," said Downer. "I think it would be worth trying anyway, though." Under his breath he started to hum a Ratty-Rat-Rat tune.

Oh Rat of better raincoats,
Of raisins and raviolis,
Oh Rat of ramifications
and grafting onto orange trees.

The deer set down his bowl of Love Noodles. Tears appeared in his eyes, which he hoofed away. But no one noticed. Our friends by now were lying on their backs and looking up at the sky.

"Too bad there's no billboards in the sky," Downer said. "I used to think, *If only I could post a correction on the moon.*"

"Or an apology," Gogo said. "Sometimes I want to post a little apology up there."

The deer wiped his eyes with his front haunch.

"How do they know which ones aren't stars?" Fred asked. "I mean, which ones are planets, and which are stars?"

"I've been sleeping under the stars my whole life and I still don't know which ones are planets," Downer said.

"The planets are the ones that don't twinkle," the deer said quietly.

"Huh?"

"Planets give off a steady light. And stars do that glittery thing," the deer said. "My mom taught me that."

"You're saying the stars are like candles and the planets are like night-lights?" Fred asked.

"I like that," the deer said. "That's Sirius, for example," he added, pointing.

"Oh, I don't mean to be so serious," Downer said.

"Not serious like so," the deer said, pulling a serious face that made them laugh. "I mean Sirius *the star*. The Dog Star. That one."

The star at one moment seemed blue, another moment pink, another moment golden white.

"Sirius is actually two stars. It only looks like one," the deer said.

Fred said, "You mean, it's two locked boxes. And each contains the other's key?"

"I don't know about that," the deer said. "I mean it's two dwarfs burning."

"No violence in front of the child, please," said Gogo.

"Two dwarf *stars* burning," the deer said.

"I know what a dwarf star is," Fred said. Though she didn't really know what dwarf stars were; she had only heard the phrase. But she would learn one day, she felt certain.

"You know, it's funny," the deer said. "All this talk about stars makes me really miss my mom."

"That puts them to sleep," Fred said, with a small laugh. "When we were trying to get to the Land You Can Only Get to Through Sleep, I told them about *my* mom. It worked like a charm."

The deer looked more closely at the three friends. "Why were you going to The Land You Can Only Get to Through Sleep?"

Fred yawned. "We were looking for the Rat then. Now we're looking for someone else. But we can't tell you what we learned about the Rat. We're not supposed to let the cat out of the bag." She stretched.

"Let what cat out of the bag?" asked the deer.

No one was listening. Have you ever eaten a lot of noodles? One magic property of even ordinary noodles, let alone Irrational Love Noodles, is that they make you sleepy and contented. They don't even give you a tummy ache. They just make you feel like everything in the world is fine. Sometimes they help you Know that You Are Loved. When Gogo poured water on the campfire and lay down, Fred was already on Downer's forepaw, asleep.

But deer do most of their sleeping during the day, not at night.

So after a few more moments of looking up at the stars, the deer walked quietly away.

Now you may be thinking something. And what you are thinking is right. This deer was Hart. Sometimes you find things by no longer searching. And sometimes you find things and you have no idea that you found them and then they walk right back into the dark, dark woods.

Hickory Dickory

"The early bird gets the worm," a voice was saying, shaking Fred's arm, trying to wake her up. In her dream, she kept asking a cloud its name, and instead of answering the cloud kept shaking its head and saying, *It's cloudy in here!*

"But don't worry, the second mouse gets the cheese," the voice went on to say.

Fred's pajamas and slippers were damp with dew. Fred opened her eyes—was that Picky Mouse? The same Picky Mouse who had been so uninterested in their trip to find the Rat? What was *he* doing *here*? He said, "It's already 7:16 a.m. Soon it's going to be 7:17 a.m. After that 7:18 a.m. is going to be coming after you."

The cuckoo clock, in the morning sun, looked more beautiful than when they had barely spied it in the dark. And it appeared to be working! There was a scent of gingerbread in the air. "What are you doing here, Picky? Aren't you supposed to be stopping time, not hickory-dickory-docking it?"

Picky Mouse shrugged. "The Rat's directive is so unclear that I both keep time and non-time. There are so many contradictions in The Essential and Very Good and No One Can Disagree with Rat Rule 79 that, well, I do what I can."

Downer was stretching nearby. Gogo was doing what looked like morning calisthenics.

Fred said, "Let me get this straight. You run the non-functioning clocktower. *And* you also run this functioning clocktower."

"More or less. Yes and No."

Gogo made her way over. "Do I smell cookies?"

Picky Mouse smiled. "Yes, it's a gingerbread clock. I baked this one. So that I could say it was Not-a-Clock. It's a Dessert. Somehow I get away with it."

Downer was inspecting a candy heart window decoration. Fred broke a bite off the ledge.

"Hey! Time-consuming is still against the rules, even here," Picky Mouse called out. "Let's not attract unnecessary attention."

"Does the Rat know about this?" Fred asked.

"Nes and Yo," said Picky Mouse. "If you know what I mean." Picky Mouse invited the friends into the Not-a-Clock-but-Dessert Tower. He set out a yellow and white check tablecloth. He put on some hot cocoa and brought out a bag of rainbow-colored mini marshmallows.

Here they were, around a table again. It was the same, and not the same.

Gogo inhaled deeply. "Bingo and Ergo and Argo would love this gingerbread. And Oswego and Manchego and Bob. Could you give me the recipe for me to try when I get home? If I get home. Logo, Pogo, and Togo used to find ginger too spicy. I wonder if they still do. Honestly, how do you keep creatures from eating your whole cuckoo clock? Do you fight them off?"

"Fred knows how I keep people away," Picky Mouse said with a mischievous smile. He stirred his cocoa and winked at her.

"I do?"

"Yes, you do," said Picky Mouse.

"I don't," said Fred.

"But also you do," said Picky Mouse. "Think about it."

"I'm trying," Fred said.

"I throw parties," Picky Mouse said.

"You do?" said Downer.

"What kind of parties?" asked Gogo.

"Show them, Fred," Picky Mouse said.

Fred blushed, realizing Picky Mouse must have known that she had stolen from him. "I'm sorry," Fred said. "I don't know why I took them." She pulled the stack of Un-Invitations from Gogo's backpack.

Housecooling Party! was written in bold letters across the top of one.

Then: *"You are Cordially Un-Invited . . ."*

There was a list of times not to come.

And things that would not be served.

Responses were Not Appreciated.

"Wait, so who gets un-invited?" Downer asked.

"Oh I un-invite everyone. I want to make sure everyone feels left out."

"Why aren't we un-invited?" asked Gogo, appearing genuinely hurt.

"I didn't know you guys would be around!" said Picky. "If I had, I would have asked you not to be."

"You invite everyone NOT to come?" clarified Fred.

"Yes."

"You know that's cuckoo, right?"

"I live in a cuckoo clock."

"True," she said.

- (-Chapter)

"**P**icky, how do you distribute these un-invitations?" Fred asked.

"The Time Flies do it for me. Usually at nothing o'clock at night," Picky Mouse said. "They have so little going on these days, they're happy for the chance to get out and about. They know how to reach everyone."

"I knew I took these invitations for a reason," Fred said. "I had a feeling about them." She didn't mention that the date on them was her very own birthday. "Here's the plan. We'll make these un-invitations into un-un-invitations. We'll send them out announcing a party—you know what kind of party—for Hart. We'll un-un-invite the Rat. We'll un-un-invite Hart. We'll un-un-invite everyone. I floated this idea by Downer and Gogo before, and we couldn't decide. It makes a crazy kind of sense, right? What do you think, Picky?"

"I'm not going to say it's a good idea," said Picky Mouse. "And I'm not going to say it's a bad idea. It's a good *and* bad idea."

"I'm hoping it's a Bood idea," said Gogo. "And not a Gad idea. Meaning it's bad now, but maybe it will be good later. Rather than the other way around."

Let me tell you, if you're as much an un-fan of suspense as I am: they went ahead with Fred's plan. The Time Flies set off on their delivery errand. Gogo took a moment to polish her Grue gems with a dishcloth. Downer sat nearby making minor repairs to his umbrella, humming a tune quietly:

The Hart of rhymes and reams and riddles
And croissant crumbs in your hair
A peanut butter and pickle-eater
Who's never ever there.

Picky Mouse was baking small gingerbread clocks; Fred was decorating them with yellow and white icing, and an occasional marshmallow. Looking up from her labor, she saw out the window those neon glowing orbs again—the Round Tuits. They appeared to be hopping nearer.

"They're beautiful, right?" said Picky Mouse, following Fred's gaze. "Very rare to see them so close," she said.

"Why is everyone so frightened of them?"

Picky Mouse shrugged. "Maybe it's spooky, never knowing when they'll arrive. Round Tuits have a famously unpredictable migration pattern. When I least expect them, there they are. Try not to be afraid of them."

The cookies looked so festive. Fred wondered who would turn up for the party—if anyone would.

"Are we doing the wrong thing?" Fred asked.

"We're doing something we haven't done before."

"Are you scared, Picky Mouse?"

"A little."

Chapter Thirteen

There were old card tables to unfold and dust, paper party hats to make, more gingerbread cookies to bake. Time flew by, even without the Time Flies, until suddenly the cuckoo clock chimed: the time had arrived.

Everything was ready.

Nobody came!

It was a surprise to see Nobody at first, but there he was, smiling, carrying Nothing. Very soon after, a line of birds approached, on foot. Their necks were mostly green, even what one might call royal green. Their chests were red, their heads were golden, and they seemed to be wearing pearl necklaces.

"The birthday pheasants!" Gogo called out joyfully. "I can hardly believe they're real." No one had seen a birthday pheasant in no one knew how long.

"Isn't that word illegal?" Fred whispered. "We don't want to, you know, steal a car on our way to robbing a bank."

Gogo was greeting the glamorous birds. She said they used to work together. "They have an exception. It's who they are, after all."

A herd of Rat-rescuing rabbits arrived next, cheerful and full of intent. One was playing a Ratty-Rat-a-Tat tune on the harmonica. Another was holding a long tube of wrapping paper, while three others were still discussing what to bring as a gift.

An inky assortment of Ferlings arrived. "We're so very happy to be here. Not that we know where we are." One tall Ferling presented as a gift a tree branch on which fortune cookies were growing.

Behind the Ferlings, silvery Insult Fish arrived, walking on their tails. "It's about time!" "No time like the present!" they carped to one another with a buoyant grouchiness. They brought flotsam and jetsam. Fred used the seaweed and bleached-out rubber duckies to decorate the tables.

Duck-Billed Platypus came next, wearing a shy smile.

Next, Badger, Penguin, and Koala from the School of Unlearning showed up! "Thank you for sending us a piece of paper with words on it that directed us to a position in time and space," Badger said.

"You mean the un-un-invitation?" Fred asked.

"Whatever you want to call it is good by me," Badger said.

Penguin and Koala nodded and called out "Yes, Ma'am!" in unison.

Behind them came the little mouse who had complained of being too big, wearing a larger version of the too-small elephant T-shirt. Picky Mouse ran up to him and covered him in hugs and kisses, exclaiming about how much she missed him, and how perfect he was just the way he was.

Old stuffed animals Fred had lost years earlier turned up, too. They were full of beans.

And you'll never believe who arrived next. Or maybe you will. Mango, Django, Tango, Bingo, Dingo, Argo, Ergo, Oswego, Durango, Manchego, Logo, Togo, Pogo, Fandango,

Quetzaltenango, Ego, and Bob. You can't imagine how happy they were to see their mom. Or maybe you can.

By the time the Rat arrived, the gathering was so crowded and jolly that at first no one noticed. There was the Rat. Dogma was at her side. The Rat looked lost, emotional, even confused. Fred approached.

"I'm so happy you're here," said Fred, as politely as she could muster.

"Oh, hello there," said Rat. She stiffly handed over a grocery bag full of confetti and glitter.

"Are you okay with . . . this?" Fred asked.

The Rat cleared her throat. "It's a perfectly lovely . . . a perfectly lovely. . . ." She coughed. "It's a perfectly lovely . . . gathering."

"Yes," agreed Dogma. "Perfectly lovely."

"It certainly doesn't appear to be a festival celebrating the passage of a year in a creature's life," observed Rat.

"Certainly not," Dogma agreed.

"If you say so," Fred said, and gave Rat a hug.

More and more creatures came. More and more and more. But.

A Hartless Chapter

Hart had still not arrived.

"We'll give him time," said Picky Mouse.

"We'll hope for the best," said Gogo.

"We love the gingerbread," said Mango and Bingo and Oswego in unison.

Downer felt differently. "He won't come. Why would he come? He probably hates parties. Especially parties with morose elephants."

The Rat's nervous smile was turning into a nervous half-smile.

Still: Fred's mom had once promised Fred she would show her how to make dumplings at home. But then the next day she didn't follow through on her promise. But then the day after that she came home with dumpling wrappers and scallions and ginger and cabbage. And they made a big batch of dumplings, each one looking like something between a hobo's bag and a perfect present. *You never know*, was what Fred was thinking, or hoping. If not now, maybe soon.

She walked with Downer to the refreshments table. It was a bountiful table, even if it had no peanut butter and pickle sandwiches on it. *There's still time,* Fred assured herself silently. *Time for Hart to arrive.* As she poured herself a cup of lemonade, one of those round glowing orbs with the unpredictable migratory pattern was there at her feet. The beautiful lint of a sunset. Smiling.

With its glowing arm, it picked up a slip of paper that in all the hubbub must have fallen from Fred's pocket. "Is this yours?" asked the creature, in its smooth, round voice.

It was Fred's Time Violation ticket.

"Oh, that's nothing!" Downer said, before Fred could react.

"That's not Nothing," said Nobody, holding a donut. "But if you'd like some—"

"Not now," whispered Fred to Nobody.

The glowing orb turned Fred's Time Violation over, inspecting it. "A court date. That's exciting. I love a court date—"

Gogo pushed her way over and grabbed the violation. "Pay that no mind! Less important than a lamppost at noon! No more than a mote in the manger! Just something we were going to think about when we got—"

The Round Tuit turned its innocent, luminescent face up at the mongoose, at the elephant, at the human girl. "Why does everyone look so afraid?"

Law and Disorder

"Her Honor Judge Kangaroo is busy," said a frowning unicorn in a long black robe. A high table had appeared from nowhere. "I will be your judge."

You might think of unicorns as sylvan creatures that nibble on buttercups in a meadow. But when a unicorn is frowning and clearing her throat while seated behind a high table, you notice the largeness of a unicorn's nostrils and teeth. You remember that a unicorn weighs more than a half-ton. You see that its horn is a sharp and strong weapon.

A Fearsome or Friendly Ferling franticked a chair over to Fred, pushing it under her from behind. She found herself sitting to the left of the unicorn's high table.

Benches were taken from the party tables and placed in rows in front of the unicorn. Round Tuits occupied the front row, and behind them sat the crowd that had come for the party. But there wasn't a party hat to be seen, nor the tooting of a party horn to be heard. Looming behind them all was the Cuckoo Clock, now like the clock of a High Court.

The gowned unicorn rapped her gavel. "The accused may sit down," she said. Unicorns have low, booming voices, by the way. A unicorn sounds like a foghorn.

Fred stayed seated.

"I said, 'The accused may sit down.'"

"I'm already sitting," Fred said as politely as she could manage. Her knees were trembling.

"Premature seat-taking. Noted." The unicorn penned something into her notebook.

"Boy, that unicorn is strict," a little mongoose voice said.

Fred looked around, hoping to find a friendly face, but the sun was shining so brightly that she couldn't make out any faces beyond the front row of Round Tuits, and even they looked blurred. She resolved not to chew on her nails, with everyone looking at her. Wait—was that a red-and-white check skirt there in the back? Or was she seeing what she hoped to see? The red vanished in a blink. Fred turned to regard the unicorn.

The unicorn gave Fred a big, toothy smile.

Maybe this would be over soon.

The unicorn rapped her gavel again and commanded, "Bring in the Jury of her Fears."

Fred thought that she'd misheard. Surely the unicorn had said "jury of her *peers*"?

Darkness came over the room as if from an eclipse. The darkness condensed into a puppy. "Dogma!" she cried out joyfully. Sweet Dogma, who had helped Fred across the Sea of Technically True Things.

But Dogma didn't answer Fred or even look in her direction, and she remembered that it was Dogma who had issued the Time Violation ticket in the first place.

Dogma led in the Jury of Fred's fears: Mushy Foods, People Who Hold Eye Contact Too Long, the Deaths of Others,

Unseen Lurking Toads, Loneliness, Ugliness, the Dark, the Kitchen Sink Drain, Lava, the Future, and several Unnameable Shapes for which Fred couldn't find a description, though she recognized them.

Fred began to chew on her nails.

The unicorn shuffled awkwardly through the papers on her bench. Having hooves makes paperwork tricky. "It says here that you planned to get older and wiser? Is that correct?"

"Um, I wouldn't use the word *planned*," Fred said. Her eyes had begun to adjust to the bright light. She looked again into the far corner, where she earlier might have seen red-and-white checks, and for a second she made out . . . her mom?

But this woman didn't seem perturbed at all. Just interested. As if she were watching a nature documentary or a juggling act. Also, there was a bird—an owl, Fred now saw—perched on her shoulder. And the longer Fred looked, the clearer it became that the red-and-white-skirted shape wasn't a woman at all, but only an upholstered chair.

"Excuse me!" shouted the voice of Gogo. "Excuse me, Your Honor!"

Fred scanned the audience and spotted her—on Downer's back, along with her seventeen children. She had converted Downer's umbrella into a kind of megaphone. "Your Honor! The accused is entitled to counsel!"

An owlish shadow passed silently over the courtroom. It came to rest on Fred's chair with a confident posture that, to be honest, was really annoying.

It was the Know-It-Owl!

RIVKA GALCHEN

"I represent the accused," the Know-It-Owl declared. Her spotted feathers looked humbly magnificent, like the seed pattern in a kiwi. She spread her wings wide and held them open for three long, very dramatic seconds. Fred felt a surge of well-being. Those wings had once seemed menacing; now they seemed protective.

The Know-It-Owl folded her wings. She said, "Your Honor, I have a preliminary point."

A whispering passed through the crowd. There is nothing like a preliminary point to get people excited.

"What is your preliminary point?" the unicorn said.

"Unicorns don't exist, Your Honor."

"What?" snorted the unicorn.

"Allow me to rephrase that," said the Know-It-Owl. "*It is not strictly true* that unicorns exist. That is my client's position."

The unicorn judge smiled. "Well, I exist, don't I?"

"Up to a point, Your Honor." The Know-It-Owl somehow produced a dictionary from her wings. She showed the judge the definition of "unicorn." "Your Honor is a *mythical animal.*"

"Yes," the unicorn judge admitted grumpily. "It does say that."

"Perhaps Your Honor could look up 'mythical.'"

The unicorn read out, "Occurring in myths or folktales."

"Perhaps Your Honor could look up 'myth.'"

The unicorn hoofed the dictionary back at the Know-It-Owl. "I get it, counselor. What is your point?"

"My point is this: Your Honor does not *strictly* exist."

222

A rumble of astonishment passed through the courtroom. Mixed in with the rumble was a sort of flappy wet sound. Fred realized that the Insult Fish were clapping.

The unicorn huffed through her nostrils. "Technically, that would be true. Strictly speaking."

The Know-It-Owl turned to the jury. "You heard the judge. Her Honor doesn't exist, strictly speaking. And in this court we speak strictly or not at all." The Know-It-Owl spread her wings again. Rather proudly, it must be said. "If there is no judge," the Know-It-Owl declared, "there can be no judgment."

Fred started gnawing on a corner of her right thumbnail. Being rude to the judge didn't strike her as a great strategy.

The unicorn rose. "All rise!" cried Dogma.

Fred stood up. Everyone in the courtroom stood up, even the Insult Fish. The unicorn announced, in a quiet and yet booming voice, "I must concede counsel's point. I do not exist, strictly speaking. Which means that this trial does not exist and has never existed."

To muffled cheers and grumbles, the unicorn stepped down. Fred's Fears began to leave their seats.

Until a new voice spoke. "Hold your horses!"

A Pegasus had taken the unicorn's place. Also wearing a judge's robes. A Pegasus, of course, is a horse that is winged but not horned. A Pegasus has a much higher, more horse-like voice than a unicorn, and sort of whinnies out words.

"Uh-oh," the Know-It-Owl whispered. "I hoped there would be no backup judge."

The Fears reseated themselves.

"I know what y'all are going say: I'm a mythical animal, too," drawled the Pegasus. "But let's get real, folks. All that about mythical animals not existing? Why, it just don't make a lick of horse sense. Little lady, this case will proceed."

The owl whispered into Fred's ear, "Don't worry, I have a million strategies. A million and nineteen, even."

Horse Sense

It's amazing how bad something can sound when it's announced in official language. *The accused, following a plan to . . . incited others to . . . thereby initiating a return of . . . furthermore engaging others as . . . in violation of The Essential and Very Good and No One Can Disagree with Rat Rule 79.*

Fred found it unbearable. Fred's Fears, though, leaned in to listen.

When the Pegasus finished reading the charge, he was silent for a moment. Then, slowly, dramatically, he spread *his* wings and held them out. A squawk of admiration and awe sounded in the audience. A flying horse has enormous wings. Think about how heavy a horse is, and how much power it needs to get airborne. That's a lot of plumage.

The Know-It-Owl bravely said: "Thank you, Your Honor. Most helpful. Now: could I ask Your Honor to look at the Time Violation ticket?"

Dogma passed the ticket to the judge.

The Know-It-Owl continued, "You'll see there is a time stamp on the ticket. That tells you precisely when the accused's comments were made, in Rat Standard Time. What does the time-stamp say, Your Honor?"

"11:21 p.m.," said the winged judicial horse. "That ain't

exactly surprising, Owl. It's been 11:21 p.m. for as long I can remember. Since the Rat *made* Rule 79."

"Indeed, Your Honor," Know-It-Owl said. "When the Rat stopped the clocks, time stood still at 11:21 p.m. It was only when the Hart's birthday party began that Rat Standard Time began ticking again. Illegally, of course."

"Get to the point, Owl," the Pegasus said.

The Know-It-Owl addressed the jury of Fred's Fears. "Here's the question: If you have a cup and then put a handle on it, is it still a cup? If you have a sock puppet with a frog face on it, then replace that frog face with a monkey face, do you still have a frog puppet?"

The Pegasus said, "Owl, you've plumb lost me."

"It is *not* the same cup! It is *not* the same puppet. What was a handleless cup is now a mug! What was a sock-frog puppet is now a sock-monkey puppet."

"Or a sock-fronkey puppet," said Fred, but nobody paid her any attention.

Pegasus said, "Owl, I'm fixin' to hold you in contempt of court. The folks of the jury"—he indicated Fred's Fears— "have better things to do than listen to mumbo jumbo."

The Know-It-Owl stood her ground. "All will become clear, Your Honor, in the fullness of time. I have a question for the accused. Miss Fred, do your fingernails grow?"

The jury leaned in closer.

"I assume they do," Fred cautiously answered. She had never actually *seen* them growing.

"And have you ever cut or abridged your fingernails?"

Fred hesitated. What did "abridge" mean?

"Are you in the habit of shortening your nails with your teeth?" ventured the Know-It-Owl.

"I have, umm, been known to abridge my nails with my teeth," she admitted.

"And did you abridge your fingernails in this courtroom today?"

Again Fred hesitated.

"Did you not just one minute ago chew on your fingernails, Fred?"

She felt embarrassed and betrayed. The Know-It-Owl was supposed to be on her side! "I did," Fred admitted.

"Excellent." The Know-It-Owl opened her wings to their fullest extent and then said, in a loud hooting voice that startled everybody into attention: "The girl we see here on trial today—that girl!—is not the same girl as the one who was issued a ticket. And here is the proof." The Know-It-Owl held out Fred's hand, chewed fingernails prominent.

There was a gasp from the audience.

Waving the violation ticket with one wing, the Know-It-Owl declared: "The person who received this ticket was a girl named Fred at 11:21 p.m. with fingernails in the 11:21 p.m. state. The girl before us here today is Fred at 11:43 p.m. with 11:43 p.m. fingernails. Those fingernails are shorter now than they were at 11.21 p.m. *They're different fingernails.*"

"What in the heck are you saying, Owl?" the judge asked.

"I'm saying that the 11:21p.m. version of Fred may well be guilty of violating Rat Rule 79. But *that was a different*

Fred. This Fred, Your Honor"—the Know-It-Owl gestured dramatically—"*this* Fred, the accused, is not guilty. What we have here is a case of mistaken identity."

The Pegasus said, "Are you kidding me?"

But the crowd shouted, "Not Guilty, Your Honor! Not Guilty! Mistaken identity! Not Guilty!" And the jury nodded in agreement with the crowd. The judge nickered and said to Fred: "Looks like you did it, kid. You beat the rap."

Gogo let out a cheering yawp, and Django and Durango and Ergo and Argo and the rest of the gang cheered as well. Downer wiped a tear from his eye. Fred was free to go!

A Hartfelt Chapter

"**O**bjection, Your Honor!"

The Pegasus rapped his gavel again. "Whoa, everybody. Whoa."

"Objection, Your Honor," the voice from the audience repeated.

It was a sweet voice. And young. But not very young.

Hart! Fred thought joyfully. Hart has arrived!

"Step up and state your objection, young sir," commanded the robed flying horse.

Hart elegantly trotted forward. "11:43 p.m. Fred *is* the same person as the 11:21 p.m. Fred," Hart said. "It doesn't matter how long or short her nails are. It doesn't matter how old or young she is. Fred is Fred. We know it in our hearts."

Fred's heart sank. In her heart, she agreed with Hart. She stood up and at long last spoke for herself. "Hart is right. What the hart is saying is what I think, too."

A shocked murmur rippled through the crowd. Pegasus said, "Little lady, you just admitted that you broke the law. You got anything to add, Owl?"

The Know-It-Owl sat quietly. She also knew Hart had a point.

"Not so fast, Your Honor," Hart said with dignified calm. The room was silent.

"Your Honor," Hart continued quietly, "Rat Rule 79 requires Fred to not grow up. But that's asking the impossible. Fred is a kid. Kids grow up. They can't help it. And you can't be guilty of a failure to do the impossible."

"Why not?" asked the Pegasus judge.

Hart replied, "Because the girl has done no wrong. It's Rat Rule 79 that's in the wrong here. It's not essential, it's not at all good, and I disagree with it."

There were gasps. Even the judge gasped.

"That's what I wanted to say," Hart said. "Also: when I was a stranger, Fred and her friends shared their Irrational Love Noodles with me."

Hart stood his ground.

There was a loud scuffling and clattering—the sound of aluminum cans, orange peels, old glass bottles. The mongeese were suddenly streaming down from Downer's back. Onto which the Rat had climbed up. She was still in her shabby robe. But she seemed to have a dignity within her. She seemed, again, like a Queen.

From above, she looked around. Would she be angry? Vengeful? Hurt? Would there be a New Law?

The Rat coughed.

The Fears leaned in.

Picky Mouse checked his watch.

Dogma stood at attention.

The rabbits were at the ready.

The fish held their breath.

The Ferlings were flushed.

The Unlearning students covered their ears but kept their eyes open.

The Rat took a deep breath and said: "I owe you all an apology." She coughed again. "I was wrong. Very wrong. I'm sorry about Rat Rule 79. It was stupid. It is not true that Too Many Birthdays Can Kill You. It only sounds true. I took unfair advantage of that. The truth is that The Person Who Has the Most Birthdays Lives the Longest."

Clapping and cheering and even party horn tooting erupted from the audience.

"And to you, Hart, I especially owe an apology. I am so proud of the deer you have grown up to be. I loved you when I met you, I loved you as you were at 11:21 p.m., and I love you now, and I will love you forever. Happy birthday."

Hart approached the Rat, and the Rat scurried across Downer's back and down his trunk and approached Hart. They hugged.

Then the Rat climbed up onto Hart's back and shouted: "For the avoidance of doubt and further heartbreak, I declare Rat Rule 79 to be null and void!"

The Pegasus rapped the gavel with great enthusiasm. "Yippee! Time is hereby un-adjourned! Folks of the jury, you are discharged. Fred, getting older is no longer a crime and never was. You are free to leave and celebrate your birthday. I declare as follows, by golly: it's time for cake."

Another Surprising Dungeon Chapter Without Assigned Number

The room was the same, but also not the same. There was the cheering beam of sunlight. The high, penny-colored bars. The mysterious pile of hay. And the white elephant. Only Fred didn't think of him as a white elephant anymore, of course; he was Downer, her friend.

"Downer, why are we here? Why aren't we at the party?"

Downer said nothing.

Fred said, "If I'm not guilty, why aren't I . . . free?"

Downer replied, "Ever had one of those dreams where you can decide how the dream goes?"

"You're not in my dream, Downer. I tried that already, a long time ago. You're real."

"Thanks," Downer said.

Fred smelled the hay. Touched the walls. Pushed at the door. Climbed up onto Downer's back to look out the high window.

"I'm back to square one. It's hopeless," Fred said.

Downer shook his head. "That sounds like me, not like you. All this time you've been working to find your mom and get back home. Or so you say. Maybe you didn't really want to go there."

"That's crazy. Of course I want to go home. There's no place like home."

Downer said, "If you say so."

"Though I guess, now that I've spent so much time here, I know this place better than I know my new home. Leaving would make me sad."

Downer said nothing.

"Where's Gogo?" Fred asked.

"She's back home with her family. Her Grue stones are valuable again."

"Picky Mouse?"

"He has time on his hands."

"The creatures at the School of Unlearning?"

"They're unlearning so much they'll soon graduate back to learning."

"And Nobody? He was so nice to me."

"There's a renewed demand for Nothing. He's back in business."

"What about you?"

Downer blushed. "What about me?"

"Do you have what . . . what you want?"

Downer shrugged. "I freed the Rat. But that wasn't what I wanted, I've learned. What I wanted was a true friend. And now I've got one."

Fred and Downer hugged.

Fred said, "Downer, I still feel sad. Where's my mom?"

Chapter One

One oversized fortune cookie remained. Downer presented it to Fred with a flourish: "Happy birthday, my dear friend."

Now the best part about fortune cookies, as you most certainly know, is not the cookie but the fortune inside. But what would the fortune inside that giant cookie say?

Maybe I LOVE YOU.

Or YOU'RE A SWEET COOKIE, TOO.

Perhaps PLEASE DON'T EAT MY HOUSE.

There were more possibilities than names that aren't Rumpelstiltskin. But Fred didn't like suspense, and she still doesn't. This was all a while ago. You can't imagine how much older Fred is now. Or perhaps you can. Imagine if Fred was all grown up and joining the dots to tell a story to her own little Fred. A story to say *I love you as you are now and as you will be.* That would be pretty sappy, but it might also be true.

Fred quickly broke open the fortune cookie and extracted the fortune.

She laughed.

"What does it say, Fred?" Downer asked, grinning.

"It's the dumbest joke of them all. It's not even a joke, it's so dumb."

"Read it out!"

Fred read, "Knock, knock."

"Oh I love a knock, knock joke," Downer said.

And a third voice, unexpected but familiar, said: "Who's there?"

"Fred," Fred said.

"Fred who?" her mom said.

"Me, I'm a-Fred," Fred said. "Get it?"

The locked dungeon shimmered and shifted. It was still empty, but now it was empty in the way her new bedroom at home was empty. She reached for the doorknob and found that it turned, as if she herself were the key. In the next room there was a chair, and the chair was filled with her mother and her mother's laughter.

ACKNOWLEDGMENTS

So many thanks to the wildly kind and brilliant people I am lucky enough to know and work with: to my family; to Nathan Rostron and the whole team at Restless Books; to Elena Megalos; to Bill Clegg, and the whole team at the Clegg Agency; also thank you to my earliest readers, Joseph O'Neill and Michael Fields.

This book owes an especial debt to the many marvelous writers in the long tradition of nonsense and logic.

ABOUT THE AUTHOR

RIVKA GALCHEN is an award-winning fiction writer and journalist who loves noodles and numbers and modest-sized towns where her dad might have worked. Her work appears often in the *New Yorker, Harper's,* the *London Review of Books* and the *New York Times.* She is the author of three books: *Atmospheric Disturbances* (novel, FSG, 2008), *American Innovations* (short stories, FSG, 2014) and *Little Labors* (Essays, New Directions, 2016). She has received numerous prizes and fellowships, including a Guggenheim Fellowship, a Rona Jaffe Foundation fellowship, the Berlin Prize and the William Saroyan International Prize in Fiction. In 2010, she was named in the *New Yorker*'s list of 20 Writers Under 40. Galchen also holds an MD from the Mount Sinai School of Medicine. *Rat Rule 79* is her first book for young readers.

ABOUT THE ILLUSTRATOR

ELENA MEGALOS was raised in the City of Angels. When she was twelve going on thirteen she dreamed of writing the cookie fortunes for her beloved neighborhood Chinese restaurant, The Unicorn. That, or illustrating a book for children. This is her first one. See more work at elenamegalos.com.

Yonder is an imprint from Restless Books devoted to bringing the wealth of great stories from around the globe to English-reading children, middle graders, and young adults. Books from other countries, cultures, viewpoints, and storytelling traditions can open up a universe of possibility, and the wider our view, the more powerfully books enrich and expand us. In an increasingly complex, globalized world, stories are potent vehicles of empathy. We believe it is essential to teach our kids to place themselves in the shoes of others beyond their communities, and instill in them a lifelong curiosity about the world and their place in it. Through publishing a diverse array of transporting stories, Yonder nurtures the next generation of savvy global citizens and lifelong readers.

Discover more at restlessbooks.org/yonder.